THE SACRED WOOD

KEVIN D. FINSON

Dedicated to Ellen for her steadfast faith and constant prayers.

© by Finson, 2025. All rights reserved.

No part of this publication may be reproduced or used in any form or by any means, electronic or mechanical, including photocopying, recording, or by any information storage and retrieval system, without the express written permission from the copyright owner. For information regarding permission, write to: **kevindfinsonauthor@gmail.com**.

Independently Published. ISBN 979-8-9927381-0-0

The Sacred Wood

Table of Contents

Chapter	Title	Page
1	The Old Rocking Chair	1
2	Grandma and the Stories	7
3	The Family in the Old Country	13
4	The Family in the New Country	21
5	The Mountain Decision	31
6	Finding the Mountain	41
7	Through the Pass	53
8	The New Homestead Place	59
9	Pulling Up Old Roots for New Ones	67
10	The Stories of the Wood	75
11	Cross Wood	91

The Sacred Wood

CHAPTER 1

The Old Rocking Chair

The old rocking chair sat in its place on the porch of the log cabin. Nothing else had occupied that spot for as long as anyone could remember. The floorboards of the porch were a dusty brown, and the occasional knothole allowed one to peek down into the crawlspace beneath it. Children often peered down through the knotholes thinking they might see some treasure twinkling in the shadowy space below, but the reality was just critters hiding under the boards peering upward at the spots of sunlight poking through the openings. Usually, the critters were dogs hiding from the heat of the summer's day, or the occasional racoon hoping to snag a tasty meal from tidbits left unguarded by the folks who lived in the cabin. Rare occasions saw an opossum resting down there, and every once in a while, a cottontail rabbit would scamper along trails hidden beneath the porch boards.

Some of the porch floor planks had cupped, or curved down along their center lengths. Part of that was caused from using wood that had not had sufficient time to dry and season before being used. Small ridges formed where the edges of the planks met each other, but they had been smoothed and rounded from years of footwear moving back and forth over them.

The rocking chair's gently curved rockers seemed to fit nicely into the middle of two planks near one end of the porch just past the cabin's front door. Everyone knew the rocking chair was very old. In fact, it had been made from wood harvested from trees that once stood where the cabin now rested.

The cabin itself was about a hundred years old. The logs of the cabin walls were once the trees that shaded that spot so long ago. Those trees were stately and exceptionally tall when Great Grandpa and his brothers first found their way into the wooded grove all those years past. They were the first settlers to reach that remote place high up on the mountain. And they took great care to fell the trees they needed without damaging other trees in the grove. They only harvested what was needed, nothing more. Great Grandpa often spoke of the majestic trees of the mountain wood. He always taught that those trees should be respected and honored for what they gave to him and his family. Those trees gave their lives so the family could have safe shelter. It was those same trees that provided comfort in many ways, from the large logs used to construct the walls of cabins to the logs split to make floorboards and roofing. Some gave their warmth in the fires kept burning in the stone hearths within the cabins. And still others gave of themselves for the wood used for the family's furniture. The remaining trees of the wood, and on the mountains around it, provided homes for the animals the family relied upon for food and pelts, as well as shade from the hot summer sun and breaks from the harsh winter winds.

Great Grandpa and his brothers arrived in the wooded grove in early spring that first year, just after the snows had melted and opened the passes enough for folks to migrate up into the mountains from the valleys below. It was important to arrive early so all the work could be done that was necessary to establish the homestead before those snows returned in the mid-autumn. Great Grandpa and his brothers made several cabins that first year, one for each of their families. None were particularly large, but each was large enough to comfortably shelter a family. Together, the cabins created a very small village, as if several cabins could constitute a village. The cabins were spread just far enough apart from each other so the trees left standing in the wood created a veil that hid one from the other, yet they were close enough that someone's calls from one cabin could easily be heard at the others. The critical thing was for the cabins to be built and ready before the snows returned.

The wood grove on the mountain had a broad variety of trees. The men harvested yellow pine and poplar for most of their cabin logs since it holds up well and resists decay, making it a good choice for cabin walls. They are strong woods and grow straight and tall. Great Grandpa and his brothers first harvested trees that had died and dried naturally so there would be less shrinkage in them once put together as cabins. Their choice for door and window frames was Western red cedar, and it was their choice for the shingles, as well. Cedar could resist moisture nicely, so it was a good choice for those purposes. There were some oaks and maple trees on the mountain, too, but those could be used for other things the families needed. Once the cabins had been constructed, Great Grandpa and his brothers were able to turn their attention to the things needed inside them. Nothing had been wasted from the tree harvest, and the smaller remnants of the trees had been carefully set aside and saved for projects such as furniture-making. And one of those projects happened to be Great Grandma's rocking chair.

Great Grandpa took his time making that furniture. He spent days sorting through the tree limbs and branches that had been saved, seeking those that were either just the right size or shape for his needs. Great Grandma often teased him about the way he would rustle through the pile, pull out one branch and hold it up as he closely examined it with a squinted eye. Her teasing did not deter him, and he would just say he had to find the pieces that were calling out to be made into one piece of furniture or another. To him, those pieces had to have a will to fit together . . . and then hold tightly to one another. He sometimes spoke about those pieces of furniture as if they were family – holding fast together to be strong and able to endure long years of wear that were ahead of them – each part providing support and strength to each of the other parts. Great Grandpa had decided to craft the rocking chair from oak. It was a hardy wood with a fine grain and a rich color.

When Great Grandpa had selected the pieces of wood for the rocking chair, he carefully removed any tiny branches or twigs – those only useful for kindling to start a fire – and then scraped off the bark from each one without gouging the heartwood beneath it. It was the heartwood that gave each piece its strength. After removing the bark, Great Grandpa began smoothing each piece to remove imperfections and rough spots. Oddly, he left many of the bumps and nubs that remained from where smaller twigs had sprouted out from a branch. He carefully smoothed the ends and gently sanded their sides so they blended gently into the main branch of the wood. He sometimes would say those bumps and nubs were not imperfections, but were the character of the wood. It was those bumps and nubs, along with the knots and grain patterns, that allowed the wood to tell its story of life to anyone who cared taking time to really look at it.

As Great Grandpa studied each branch, some seemed perfect in size and shape for specific parts of the rocking chair he was going to make. Longer flatter ones would be good for the chair's arms and back slats. It was best if the ones for the arms had a slight dip in their centers to better fit the curvature of Great Grandma's arms and elbows when she would sit in the chair. The wood for the back slats also were best if they had a slight curve, but different from the arms. Great Grandpa helped the wood out by shaping it some with his wood-working and carving tools.

The rocking chair legs had to be stout without being too thick. The seat of the chair came from a cross-cut slice of a tree trunk. It had to be just the right width to fit someone sitting on it and to give the chair stability in width. Great Grandpa took the longest time working on that piece, carefully scraping and carving out some wood here and there until the seat had a gentle dip in its center and broad yet shallow grooves to fit someone's legs. It was smoothed and shaped to mold closely to a person's body. Great Grandma was often called upon to sit on it so Great Grandpa could note where more wood needed to be removed or smoothed.

Last came the rocking chair's rungs and rockers. The rungs had to be straight and thin, yet strong. And the rockers had to be extra strong and given more curve than either the back slats or arms. Great Grandpa carefully drilled out holes and rounded the ends of certain pieces so they could be fit together into a cohesive whole – the rocking chair. Each piece gave the rocking chair strength and durability, and each supported -- in some way -- the other pieces. It was evident Great Grandpa had taken great care and employed very skillful craftsmanship to give those tree parts new life as a piece of furniture.

Over the years, certain parts of the rocking chair's wood had taken on a dark burnished brown patina where wear and tear were most pronounced. That was the seat, the arms, and part of the back of the chair. If one looked closely at the arms, the places where Great Grandma's hands had rested almost seemed to reflect the very shape of her hands. The edges of the rockers had smoothed more and become slightly more rounded from rocking so many times. The pattern of the woodgrain in each piece of wood squiggled back and forth through it as if the sap in it was still trying to move along its length. But the sap had long ago dried and left the chair.

It was a sturdy chair and had withstood uncountable sittings. Many a child had been rocked in it while cradled in the loving arms of their mothers through long nights, through illnesses, or just to provide comfort. Many a song had been hummed or sang as someone sitting in it stitched or knitted something for a loved member of the family. Many a worry had dispelled itself through its gentle rocking back and forth. Many an hour had passed with someone sitting in it watching the flames and embers in the fireplace while thinking and pondering and dreaming.

Looking at the rocking chair gave one the feeling it had seen many years of hard yet loving labor. This was Great Grandma's rocking chair. It was the first piece of furniture Great Grandpa made after the cabin was raised. Most of the other furniture in the cabin matched it to some degree, and each piece in some way paid homage to the trees that gave of themselves so such furniture could exist. But none of the furniture seemed to be as cherished as that rocking chair. None seemed to be as important. None seemed to hold within it the same depth of memories or love. Great Grandma had long since departed, as had Great Grandpa, so the rocking chair was now Grandma's. In time, it would be Momma's, and later her daughter's.

CHAPTER 2

Grandma and the Stories

    Grandma was slower these past few years. Moving from one point to another seemed to be increasingly difficult for her, yet she never complained or gave any evidence it bothered her. Rheumatism, she called it. Sometimes, she just said her joints were being extra creaky. She would turn her back to the old rocking chair, and reach back with her hands until they gripped the arms of the chair. Then she would slowly lower herself into the chair's seat and scootch backward until her back met the chair's back slats. She would often smile as the old rocking chair creaked, and would sometimes whisper, "Oh, stop yer groanin', you ol' girl!" Grandma's gnarled hands and fingers would gently wrap themselves around the ends of the rocking chair's arms. One could almost imagine that her arms and hands had melded into and matched the gnarls in the wood. She would gently straighten her apron across her knees, then tilt back her head, and with a small smile take in a deep breath. With an almost imperceptible push of her legs and feet, that old rocking chair would begin slowly swaying back and forth, its rockers pressing on the porch boards and causing them to sing softly and sweetly with the creaky song from the old chair itself.

    More and more of her time was spent sitting in the old rocking chair, letting the mountain breezes caress her face as she listened to the skitter of small animals amongst the trees surrounding the cabin – or beneath the porch boards. She particularly enjoyed watching several squirrels chase each other up and down and around the trunks and branches of some nearby trees. The trees seemed full of birds that serenaded Grandma whenever she was out on the porch. And although Papa didn't want them there, Grandma seemed to have some special friends looking a lot like raccoons who would visit her from under the porch. The old hound dog would flop down on the floor next to the rocking chair, more interested in having a snooze with some soft snoring than chasing away any critters under the porch.

Grandma always seemed to have a project of some sort going on. A project might be helping Momma clean some vegetables or fruit for a meal or in preparation for preserving them. Another might be stitching some cross-stitch. Her hands and fingers were not as nimble as they once were, yet she willed her fingers to move deftly and her stitches were always tight and perfect. As the years passed, Grandma's projects would extend to more and more time on their way to completion. Momma teased her that those projects could be done more quickly if Grandma refrained from taking so many short naps between stitches! Grandma would reply with a soft giggle.

Yet even as much as it seemed Grandma was slowing down, she always seemed to somehow be filled with some mystical energy source during evenings when everyone was gathered on the porch after supper just as the sun was finishing its course across the sky. Shadows of the trees would walk across the porch as the sun moved lower and lower toward the backside of the mountain beyond the cabin. The serenade of the birds gave way to the chirping music of crickets and other insects out amongst the grass and trees. The squirrels were at rest, and that old hound dog kept up his soft snoring next to Grandma's rocking chair. It was during these times when everyone shared something about their day or something wished for. It was during these times when joyous songs would accompany the strum of a guitar or plucking of a dulcimer, and laughter and snickers wafted from one end of the porch to the other. It was during these times when everyone might sit together in silence and let the quiet of the mountain seep in all around them.

Grandma enjoyed teaching the children songs she had learned

from her childhood. She never seemed to lack for a song no one had heard before. Yet, somehow, they fit nicely with the tunes Grandpa and Papa knew for the guitar and dulcimer. The songs always came after the time of sharing. And once the songs subsided, the quiet times came. Not long after that came the time for stories. Story time would begin as the last rays of the sun reached upward from the mountain peak and gave themselves up to the twilight. It continued into the darkening of the evening and well into when the stars had awakened in the sky overhead. Sometimes, the light from the moon would poke through breaks in the tree canopy and cast its light across the porch and seemingly halt the night's progression as stories continued to flow.

The range of story topics and types of stories varied a great deal. One story might be about a certain animal in the mountains, or one of the animals calling the cabin home. Another might be about the changing of the seasons, while another might be about the creatures envisioned in the constellations of stars above. There were stories about adventures someone had had or heard from somebody else. Some stories were about people someone knew, especially about pioneers and heroes. Once in a while, Grandpa would share a scary story, only to be chided by Grandma about scaring the children before bedtime. Some of the funniest stories were about somebody trying out a "new" food recipe and the ensuing disaster when it was served to the family. Throughout the week, everyone was given a chance to tell a story at some point. One of the most fun story times was when somebody began with a sentence, and the next person added to that sentence, and then the next person added to that second sentence, and so on. It was always impossible to predict where such a story would be going or how it might end. Usually, they ended when Momma declared it was time for bed.

Perhaps the most interesting story times were when Grandma shared something about the family's history. These were the quietest story times because nobody wanted to miss any detail she might share. Most of the time, Grandma's stories started when someone asked a question about the family or its history and she gave the answer. And the answer was always a story. It never seemed she came to story time without a story already prepared to share. They just flowed from her vast memory and experiences in her life and from what she had learned about her predecessors from her parents and grandparents. What she shared in her stories always seemed to have a moral lesson embedded in them somewhere. They always seemed to instill pride in the family. And at times, they gave everyone pause and reason to be humbled. There was always a thankful air to her stories, even when they involved tragedy of some kind. Her stories brought a richness to life and an understanding of how to better live it.

Grandpa had stories, too, but always deferred to Grandma whenever possible. He would say she was the family historian, and knew much more about the family history than he did. Grandma would then say it was just because she could remember more than he did. He would chuckle, and then sit quietly awaiting Grandma's next tale. Even so, Grandpa often encouraged the children to pay close attention and learn, because some of them would someday need to be the family historians. It was important knowledge that should not ever be lost. It was a bond with their past. He would explain how knowing and understanding their past could explain where they were now in life, why things were the way they were, and why certain things were done the way they were done. Family strength built upon what ancestors had accomplished and passed on down through the generations. And those same family history stories could point the way to the future for them. What was learned through those stories continued to build strong foundations for life yet to come.

Papa and Momma would sometimes share stories that were about family history, too. But their stories seemed to differ from Grandpa's and Grandma's. Papa's and Momma's stories were more about how they had been able to accomplish something, even if it was small and not very grandiose. The themes seemed to focus on what they had learned from family who had come before – even generations earlier -- and how that learning enabled them to succeed in the tasks that lay before them.

If a story contest was to be held, the sure winners would be Grandpa and Grandma. It depended somewhat on what the story was about. But when it came to a family history story, Grandma was hands-down the best. She just had a special way with her words. Her phrases would intertwine and yet not get lost in one another. Each phrase seemed as important as the last or the next. It was always as if one was on a journey, not quite knowing exactly where it would end, but the anticipation and excitement of the journey itself would always hang in one's ears and pull on the heart. For emphasis, she might lean forward and speak softly – at times almost at a whisper -- or straighten her back and throw up her arms with words so forceful and loud they startled everyone. The movement of her hands helped shape the tales in the mind's eye. Sometimes, the end could be seen before arriving there, but more often than not Grandma skillfully kept the ending as a surprise. There was always a twinkle in her eyes, and that twinkle would turn to a sparkle as those surprises were revealed. Even when she was asked to retell a story previously shared, she had a way of reworking it so it came out like something new. And it all seemed to be effortless for her, and flowed smoothly like the evening breeze across the porch or the trickle of the water in the mountain brook not far from the cabins.

CHAPTER 3

The Family in the Old Country

Grandma's old rocking chair and the family had moved indoors for the winter and huddled around the fireplace while wrapped in hand-stitched shawls and quilts. It was in the depths of the winter during one of those story-telling sessions that Grandma was asked about where the past family had come from. She stared into the flames and embers. Then she looked up above the fireplace mantel at the cross hanging there. That cross had been in the family for generations. It had been hand-carved by a family craftsman in the earliest years of the family. It was the most treasured item the family possessed. An elder of the family always had the honor and responsibility of caring for the cross. Although it was very old, the care it had experienced was evident. Its wood gleamed in the firelight. As Grandma looked at it, she was reminded of what it represented, and she remembered its journey along with the family through the years. She took a deep breath and pulled her quilt tightly around her shoulders. The old rocking chair was quiet as she sat there, and after a minute or so began her tale.

As with many of the people living in the region, the family initially came across the ocean from Europe. The family had deep roots there and made their homes in the mountainous areas of northern England that Grandma called "the Old Country." The mountains were rugged and so were the people who lived there. Good resources abounded for them, with plenty of wood, stone, water, and space available for living. The family was not wealthy, but was not poor by the standards of those times. They had a comfortable yet demanding life. It took a lot of work to have the necessities of life. Like most folks back then, they raised some crops and a few animals to sustain themselves.

In addition to their farming, the men of the family were well-known for their skills as craftsmen. Their craft was working with wood. Through the many generations that had come before them, they had learned the intricacies of how to work with almost any kind of wood. They had tools for harvesting, cutting, shaping, and carving. Most were tools they had made themselves, and many had been handed down from person to person through the generations. Some of the shaping tools had been so heavily used that their handles showed worn grooves where someone's fingers had grasped them over many years of using them when working wood. The family had a profound knowledge of how to wield those tools to create amazing things.

The family craftsmen were said to have so keen a knowledge of each kind of tree and how to work with its wood that it was as if the wood spoke to them. In a way, that was true. What could be fashioned one way with one kind of wood would not be workable with another kind of wood. Each wood had its own strengths, its own durability, its own character and graining and color. Each could be best used for specific purposes. A few of the older men would say that what they created from the wood was simply what was already in the wood awaiting its release. The wood spoke to them, and the good Lord guided their hands in bringing out what was deeply engrained within it.

When asked how they had gained such knowledge, they would just reply that it was their gift from God. It was something they always had, and couldn't recall anyone at any time in the family's past who wasn't so blessed. The believed they had been given the special woodworking gift so they could be good stewards of God's created mountains and forests, and so they could glorify Him by the things produced from the wood He placed upon the earth. They saw the forests and the trees as something sacred, something to be honored and cared for, and used only for good. After all, it was God's creation that they were working with.

It was said they could make something beautiful and useful out of the most ugly, gnarled pieces of wood that could be found. One ancestor said it was a reflection of the way God could take ugly, gnarled lives of people and transform them into something beautiful and useful. No matter how ugly or twisted one looked like on the outside, there was something beautifully God-given inside them. All that was necessary was for someone to masterfully bring that out. So, the men of the family saw their woodworking craft and skills as something sacred. They took great care to not do anything to the forests or to wood that would seemingly offend God. Through their work, they were honoring God and His creation.

The family's excellence in craftsmanship became known throughout the region, and eventually all throughout the country. It was not long thereafter that nobility and wealthy folks would come to the family requesting special furniture to be made. There were, of course, times when the family declined the work because of the intended use of the furniture piece. This did not sit well with certain people in high places, but the family was so admired for their work that little came of it – at first.

Then came the times when the family was asked to help construct grand houses. Back then, there were no such things as nails, and all the posts and beams for the structure of a house had to be carefully cut and joined together with wooden pins or dowels and mortise and tenon joinery. The larger the house to be built, the more massive the posts and beams needed to be. If the purpose of building such a house was for good, then the family would agree to do the task. There were, of course, times when such a task was simply for the noble or wealthy person to be extravagant and spend money they had taken as excessive taxes from the poor people living in those lands. There were also times when such extravagance would require the unnecessary clear-cutting of forests while the nobles already had other grand domiciles. Doing those kinds of projects lacked any sacredness, and often went against it. So, the family would decline to do that work. As before, this did not sit well with certain people in high places, but the family was so admired for their work that little came of it – at first.

Then came the time when the family was approached by a Cardinal of the Church and asked to help build a new cathedral. Work on the cathedral had already been underway with massive stones laid for its foundations and walls. Soon, the cathedral would need the finest of beams to support the roof, and the finest woodwork for doors, windows, and other parts of the building. And most importantly, the cathedral would need the most beautiful altar to be crafted from the finest of woods. Everything in the cathedral would be made and done to glorify God. It was a most sacred undertaking. Of course, the family agreed to take part in the construction of the cathedral. The Cardinal honored the family's decisions regarding which trees should be harvested for the work, and from where those trees would be taken. No large batch of trees was taken from any single grove or section of the woods.

The men prayed each morning, each afternoon, and each evening throughout the construction project. It seemed their hands were guided by a higher craftsman and what they produced were the most magnificent woodcrafts anyone had ever seen. The woods selected had no knots or gnarls in them. Their grain was straight and true. Their coloring was deep and rich and even throughout. Where any pieces of wood had been joined together, the joints were so straight and tight that one could scarcely tell a joint existed at all. Every piece had been hand rubbed and polished so well it reflected light almost like a mirror. Perhaps the most magnificent piece the craftsmen made was the large cross placed above the cathedral's altar. It had been modeled after the family's cross that was kept in their elder's home just above the fireplace. The cross appeared to have been made from a single piece of wood, although everyone knew it had been made from several pieces joined together. The wood appeared to be rough-hewn while at the same time being smoothed and polished so it gleamed in the light. Care had been taken to select a light-colored wood for the cross so the natural redness in the veins of its grain could easily been seen. The red veins seemed to flow outward from carved pins that looked like nails positioned just where the hands and feet of the figure of Christ were fastened to the wood. The figure was so lifelike some people felt it was ready to step forward off the cross to greet them as they approached it. Except for its size, the cathedral cross could not be distinguished from the family's home cross.

Shortly after the cathedral was finished, the King of England decreed that a new church of the state would be established, and anyone following the old Church would be punished. Some people would even be put to death for not changing their faith and attend and support the new church. The king would be the head of the new church, so anyone defying his decree would be deemed a traitor. As the king progressed in establishing his new church, he sometimes would travel the country to visit churches and cathedrals to insure the people there were following his demands. On one of his visits, he came to the new cathedral that the family had worked on. The king was stunned over the magnificence and beauty of the cathedral and thought it better than anything that existed in London. That, of course, would not do, since the best of everything should be in London -- and the best of everything should be the king's. It would be impossible to move the cathedral to London, so the decision was made to build a larger, more elaborate, more magnificent cathedral for the king's new church in London. The king desired to have the same craftsmen who built the new cathedral also build the London cathedral. He sent his men out through the countryside seeking those craftsmen. When the men of the family were found, the king's men gave them the king's decree to go to London to build the new church cathedral. There were many things about this new church that were in conflict with the family's beliefs, and the reason behind building it was not a sacred one. So, the men of the family declined to go to London.

The king's men returned to London and reported the family's decision about working on his new cathedral. Naturally, the king became enraged with the family. He proclaimed them traitors, and demanded they be found and arrested. News of the king's anger quickly reached the family before any of the king's men could find them. Before they could be captured, the members of the family packed everything they could and fled from their mountain homes. The first item they packed carefully was the family cross. Afterward came their other possessions. They sped their way to the coast, arranged to board a ship, and set sail for the New World before the king's arrest warrant could be served on them. Many weeks later, the family arrived in the New World, and set about the work of building a new home for themselves.

The New World coast was thick with trees of all kinds, and the resources for living were plentiful. The valley was lush with grasses, and just beyond the valley were hills and low mountains blanketed with trees. Wild game would quizzically approach the newly-arrived people and watch them as they went about their daily chores. Friendships were made with local native people, and the family and their companions found ways to pay the natives for the parcels of land where they would build their new homes. This new land and its resources were seen by them as a gift from God. It was a sacred place, and would be treated with the honor and respect due to that sacredness. With their craftsman skills, the family quickly forged a new and growing community for themselves and others who had fled England. Life for them was, once again, good. It was not without its difficulties, especially during the first two winters, but everyone somehow managed and soon were living comfortably. All respected the land, and pledged to only take from it what was necessary, nothing more.

CHAPTER 4

The Family in the New Country

As back in the "Old Country," the family's wood-crafting skills were well-known in their New World colony. They were called upon by many to help build their homes and shops. Much of the furniture in the colony was made by the family, and much was needed since little could be brought across the ocean from England. Most of what was brought on the ships were animals and provisions for the first year. Although there were no cathedrals to construct, the family was called upon to help build several new churches. They accepted the tasks as sacred callings, and the buildings were among the finest in the New World. Everyone thought the crosses the family created for the churches were the most beautiful parts of the buildings. The family members also lent their craft to building new boats, which were needed by colonists for fishing and navigating up and down the coast to transport goods and materials. All of this required wood, and the colonists agreed to abide by the family's guidance on careful harvesting of only certain trees in certain areas for all those needs. The colonists were following the family's example respecting and honoring the woods and resources they had been given. They were treating the land as something sacred given to them by God.

It seemed inevitable that, sooner or later, Old England would follow the New World colonists. Soon after the community had been established and was beginning to prosper, a ship arrived from England. Upon that ship was an official appointed by the King of England to be the governor of the colony. The colonists believed they had been governing themselves well enough since they set foot in the new lands, so the arrival of a new governor was not a welcome event.

Yet there was little anyone could do about it. The governor was from the king, and had been given the king's authority to govern any new colonies or settlements in the New World.

One of the first things the governor did was examine each of the houses in the community, after which he selected one for his residence and evicted the occupants. This, of course, caused quite a stir in the community, but everyone felt helpless to stop it. In the governor's eyes, the house was adequate, but was certainly beneath the quality he was duly owed according to his way of thinking.

The governor quickly determined that a new grand house be built for him. He decreed that his new house would be built on the highest hill in the colony so the view from it would look down upon everyone else. The hill the governor selected was actually just outside the community's borders, and was land that still belonged to the natives who lived in the area. The new governor did not seem to care about that. The hill was also covered by a beautiful stand of old-growth trees that were as tall and large as any back in England. All would need to be cut down to make room for the new house and the road leading up to it from the village below. Even though there were vacant lots in very good locations within the colony village, the new governor refused to build his new house on any of them. His new house had to be above all the others and set aside from the common folks and usual rabble.

On the first Sunday after his arrival in the colony, the new governor made a grand entrance into the nearest church. He was dressed in his finest fluffy garb and strutted through the front doors as if he owned the church. He seated himself in the front pew and positioned himself as if to show off his fancy clothes to everyone in the church. He scarcely paid attention to what the pastor was saying, continually fluffing his curly wig and lace collar and cuffs.

As he sat there, the governor began to notice the beautiful craftsmanship of the wooden pews, pulpit, railings, and woodwork throughout the church – and he scarcely looked at the cross. This, he thought, is exactly the kind of woodwork he wanted for his new house. He inquired of the pastor who had crafted it all, and quickly learned it was the men of the family. Instead of going to the men of the family to request they build his new house, the new governor sent one of his men with a demand they come to see him in the house he had confiscated the day he arrived in the colony. It was beneath him to take of his time to go to them. Wishing to give some respect to the governor, the men of the family went to the governor's house to meet with him. Upon their arrival, he ordered them to build his new house. Of course, knowing about the location of the hill and knowing why the governor wanted to build a new house on it, the family declined his order. There was nothing sacred or respectful about the governor's demand, and it was an intrusion into the land of their good native friends. Needless to say, the family's refusal infuriated the new governor. He repeated his demands several times over the following week, each time being declined. As before back in England, this did not sit well with the new governor or other people he had put in high places, but the family was so admired for their work that little came of it – at first. So, the beginnings of a new governor's house were at a loggerhead and delayed for many months.

Over time, the governor and his allies in the colony plotted and schemed to punish the family. They wanted to make life difficult for any member of the family for refusing the governor's demands, and sought ways to confiscate family property unjustly. For a long time, the family was able to successfully withstand the attacks that came upon them. That began to change when more ships from England arrived at the colony's shores.

On those ships were things besides provisions and new colonists. There also soldiers, tradesmen, and craftsmen. None of the craftsmen had the skills of the family, but their work could be acceptable. Under the governor's guidance, the new craftsman began by taking jobs away from the family. They would offer to do woodworking jobs for much less cost than the family could do them. Although the family did not charge large fees for their work or products, they soon found themselves losing work and not being able to sell their wares.

The governor plotted and coordinated with the new tradesmen to vote against the family in town hall meetings. Among the things they voted to do was to expand the boundaries of the colony without paying the natives for the land. They voted to clear-cut stands of trees surrounding the colony and sell the wood to other colonies. They voted to increase taxes on the properties of family members and decrease taxes on their own properties. They voted to make it illegal to make wood products the way the family had made them for centuries. They refused to sell necessities to the family for their craft. If the family objected to any of these acts, the soldiers came to intimidate them and sometimes arrested them and assessed large fines upon them. There was nothing sacred to what was happening in the colony. It was rife with evil.

Before long, the family realized they would be unable to continue living in the colony with the governor and his denizens. The pressures and attacks against them were growing almost every day, and it was just a matter of time before they would lose everything. The family sadly made the decision to depart the colony and seek another place to make their home. As they packed their belongings, one of the men went to visit their native friends living not far from the colony. The man explained the family's situation and asked the native friends for assistance in finding another place to live. He offered payment to them for the new parcel of land that would become their newest home. Soon, the man had secured the assistance he sought, had paid the natives for a piece of land, and returned to the colony to join the rest of the family. When the family members asked him where this new land was, he could not tell them, because he did not know. All he had been told by his native friends was the new land was far from the colony and had been given them by the Great Spirit. It was a place of sacredness. The native friends knew the man and the family would treat that land with respect and care. So, within the family, there was both excitement and anxiety. They were excited to have a new place to go, but were anxious about going to a place they had never seen and that was far away from people they had known for years. But they had departed the "Old Country" for new lands, and such a move was not unknown to them. They braced themselves for a hard journey and the difficulties in front of them in carving out new homesteads.

Within days, the family departed the colony and was guided to a new place by their native friends. The trail to the new land wound northward and up and through the low mountains of the coast, and then turned inland away from the ocean. It led through dense forests and woods where the trees were so thick it was difficult to see more than a couple of trees beyond the trail. The trail wound its way past rivers that whispered their burbling songs as their waters raced downslope. Their cool waters refreshed thirsty folks and were welcome respites from the heat of the day when they paused for rests. The trail passed a deep blue lake where the group paused for one night. While there, they and their native friends feasted on trout larger than any they had imagined could exist.

Two weeks passed on the trail, and then the group arrived at a broad meadow that stretched before them as far as their eyes could see. The meadow was nestled in a valley between two rows of mountains. As the wind blew through the meadow grasses, they moved like waves on the ocean. It reminded some of their journey across the ocean from the Old Country. In the distance, deer jumped and dashed through the grass into the cover of trees that bordered the meadow. Birds squealed as they took flight, startled by the movement of the family into the grasses. Beyond the edges of the meadow were mountains, rising up to meet the sky on both sides of valley. Thick forests covered the mountainsides, and there was a hint of white snow on the tips of the tallest peaks. Looking closely, one could see where a few streams seemed to appear out of the sides of the mountains and then run headlong downward toward the valley floor, forming a river that cut its way across the grasses and rushing out of the end of the valley near where they had entered it.

This was the new homeland the native friends provided them. Their native friends knew the family would treat the land with care and respect. They knew the family would honor the land and the Great Spirit that created it. They knew the family would only harvest and use what they needed, nothing more. And they also knew the family would let them hunt and travel across the valley as needed. It was a sacred place, and the family would treat it that way.

Before the first winter dusted the valley with snow, the family had built several cabins for shelter, root cellars for food storage, and a smokehouse. Those first cabins were coarse yet finely constructed. The first thing placed inside the first cabin was the family cross. The family elder positioned it above the fireplace mantel where it could be seen from anywhere in the cabin. There would be time later for the making of good furnishings for inside the new cabins. The family made some places for their animals to pasture and shelter, and cleared some plots for gardens of vegetables. Except for some hunting, few of them ventured far beyond the borders of the meadows into the mountains. Their focus was on getting settled, getting comfortable, and finding security in their new homestead.

The next couple of years were fruitful and productive for the family. They were thankful to God for what He had provided them and for their native friends. Over that time, their cabins were improved, as were their other structures, and their flocks, herds, and gardens flourished. Even so, they honored the sacredness of the land and did not over-harvest and take more than they needed. Once in a while, they enjoyed a visit from one of their native friends, or a small group of them, as they travelled through the region. It was always a joyful respite from the usual daily routines.

Then arrived a woodsman. Out from the edge of the woods at the base of the mountain he walked. He was a rough-hewn, burly individual. His coat was made of animal fur that made him look like a bear was riding on his back and shoulders. He had a hat that seemed to somehow match his coat. It made his head look extra-large while smaller at the same time. His boots were old leather with laces and straps. Despite his initial appearance, upon closer examination, one could see his beard was neatly trimmed and he was clean. He had a sparkle in his eyes as he spoke. His voice had a squeaky high tone to it, being in sharp contrast to his large size and muscular build. Someone like that would be expected to have a deep baritone voice that resonated in one's ears. That contrast was almost amusing to some children in the family.

The woodsman called himself a trail-blazer. His job was finding new trails for people to follow that would allow them to move westward to settle. He had not realized there was anyone in an established homestead this far west, and was surprised to find the family there – and living so well. He had thought this was virgin land, but had not really spoken with any of the natives in the area about the mountains or valleys there. There would be, of course, people following his trail once he returned to them and shared what he found in the mountains and the valley.

The family discussed the situation amongst themselves and then shared their concerns with the woodsman. They explained to him the agreement they had with their native friends, and anyone else who came into the valley must adhere to and abide by that agreement. There could be no deviation from it. Anyone new coming into the valley must honor it as a sacred place and only harvest and use what they needed, whether it be trees or animals or anything else. They must allow the native friends to move and hunt freely across the valley. If someone new arrived, and agreed to those terms, the family would grant them a plot of ground on which they could build their own cabin.

The woodsman stood outside a cabin and stared across the meadow down the valley and up into the bordering mountains. He rubbed his chin with his hand, back and forth, and occasionally gave off a quiet "humpf!" as he thought through things. For quite some time, he pondered what the family had told him. Eventually, he came to a decision. He would make the family's wishes known to anyone who followed the trail he blazed, and expect them to honor those wishes. However, he warned the family there might be those who would follow only part way along the trail and make their own settlements with their own rules. The family agreed that there was probably no other choice, as long as none of the new settlements encroached upon the sacred land. The next day, woodsman departed making his way back through the mountain trail he blazed earlier.

It was some months later when the first new settlers entered the valley. They were a family in search of some freedom and a new place to live. They had heard about the sacred valley from the woodsman, and were agreeable to the family's conditions for anyone living there in the valley. The family and new settlers soon had a new cabin erected on a plot of ground not far from the original family cabins. Over the ensuing months, additional settlers made their way into the valley, each agreeing to the family's conditions for living there and each getting their own plot of ground and a cabin. Years melted by, and soon the family realized their valley meadow had become crowded with other folks. All seemed to be abiding by the family's agreement with their native friends, but the number of people now living there seemed to give their end of the valley a sense of being crowded.

It was not long after when problems began to arise. People from another settlement farther back along the woodsman's trail started to infringe on the family's valley and adjacent mountains. Those people had no intention of abiding by the family's agreement with their native friends, and soon small conflicts arose over it all. The new settlers were taking more animals than necessary, and as the number of available animals decreased, the settlers expanded their hunting and trapping further and further outward from their settlements. It had started to adversely impact the population of game around the family's valley. The new settlers were cutting too many trees, and without permission from the family had started harvesting trees on the borders of the family's land. Some new settlers also moved in as squatters along the edges of the family's lands without regard for paying natives for that land, consulting the family, or acknowledging the family's agreements with their native friends. The newly-arrived folks were at times overly aggressive, greedy, and intent on having things their own way regardless of what it meant to other people. The family's native friends had been pushed out of their homes and were now living much farther away. No one in the family had seen one of them for quite some time. Disputes between the valley's inhabitants and the new settlers grew, and at times bordered on violence. There seemed to be little resolution possible. The sacredness of the valley had been violated. Once again, it seemed time for the family to move somewhere else.

CHAPTER 5

The Mountain Decision

The night had settled upon the family's cluster of cabins, as had the last snow of the winter. The air was still and blanketed the valley in its quietness. There was an occasional crack of a tree branch as it bent and broke under the weight of snow sitting on it. The crack would echo down into the valley and disappear into the darkness as the falling snow muffled its sound. The wind was still, and wood smoke hung low in the valley, wrapping itself around cabin chimneys and rooftops. Small snowflakes diffused the faint light escaping from cabin windows that had started from fireplaces in which the once-blazing fires had now calmed and were now low flames with glowing embers surrounding them. One of the cabins had some extra light shining in it. That light was from some candles resting on tables. It was in that cabin the men of the family had gathered to discuss their next move.

The candlelight flickered and caused shadows to dance across the log walls of the cabin, the door, and the furniture. The shadows seemed to exaggerate the roughness of the logs and the unevenness of the stones that made the fireplace. Even so, the light of the candles seemed to illuminate the cross hanging above the fireplace mantel, and none of the shadows seemed to rest on it. The fire in the fireplace ebbed between brightness and dimness, seeming to call attention to its need to be poked and stirred. Its flickering flames were mimicked by those of the candles.

The gathered group of men included Great Grandpa, his three brothers, and several others. Each had taken his place around the large wooden table near the kitchen space in the cabin. The glow of the fireplace illuminated the whiskers in their beards and gave their eyes some extra sparkle. But that sparkle was just in the reflections in their eyes. The men's faces were sad, and that sadness showed in the depths of their eyes. But also in those eyes was determination. That same determination resonated in their low, quiet voices as they discussed what was to come next for their families.

The table quietly creaked as some rested their elbows on it and leaned forward as they took their turns speaking. Each seemed to have come to the same conclusion: living in the valley was becoming more and more untenable. There were ever-increasing assaults on their way of living. Their native friends were no longer nearby. What had once been a place of sacredness and security had devolved into a place of unease. The men were no longer certain their families could safely live the sacred life they desired. What they had made over the years through hard work and care for the valley was now being slowly but surely taken from them.

The men sat back in their chairs around the table, glancing back and forth at each other for a couple of minutes. Some stroked their beards while others rubbed their cheeks with a couple of fingers. Following some silence, Great Grandpa spoke. It appeared their choice was to allow themselves to be subsumed within the encroaching way of life of the new settlers or to move elsewhere and start new homesteads. All the men nodded their heads in agreement. None relished the thought of altering their ways to fit in with those of the new settlers. The sacredness of life and how to live that life was too important to them. It had been ingrained deeply into each of them through many generations extending back to the Old Country. It was part of who they were. They could not abandon it. Yet moving everyone and everything to begin homesteading anew was daunting. But they were each confident that God was clearly now pointing them to do just that.

The decision of going or staying seemed to have been already decided in their minds before they gathered that night. There was no disagreement amongst them about it. One of Great Grandpa's brothers then said the question remaining was where to move the family, and when to move. The men turned to each other and began murmuring about it until Great Grandpa called them back to order and quieted the talk.

Taking their turn, a couple of the men suggested moving further down into the valley, seeking space at its far end where nobody had yet set down roots. It was so far down the long valley it looked like the point where the two bordering mountain ranges merged together. They argued that the lay of the land and the resources there would be much like what they had in this near-end of the valley, so adjusting to being there would be relatively easy. One of the brothers said none of the men disputed that point. But Great Grandpa said if that is where they re-settled, it would only be a matter of time before the new settlers' expansion would encroach upon them again. It would then be just another matter of time until another move would be necessary. The murmuring started again but quickly quieted. All seemed to turn to face Great Grandpa at the same time, and one after another spoke up in agreement with him.

After that came some silence. It seemed each of the men was pondering deeply about what that decision really meant. Some leaned forward, resting their arms on the table. Others leaned back in their chairs. The fire in the fireplace crackled, and from one of the burning logs came a pop that shot out some small embers and sparks. Great Grandpa took hold of the iron poker and stirred the logs in the fireplace. That seemed to renew the flames. And the renewed flames seemed to throw their light on the cross hanging above the mantel.

One of Great Grandpa's brothers stared at the cross for a moment and then spoke up. Up into the mountains is where they should go. High up into them. The new settlers had a laziness about them and would prefer staying in the easy living of the valley rather than up in the rugged mountain peaks. It was too hard and too difficult for them to carve out places to live up there. They just wouldn't do it. Another brother nodded in agreement as he straightened his back and added that there were just as many good resources up there as in the valley, except for a lot of good grazing land – but there were probably some mountain meadows up there they could find and use. The third brother also nodded his head in agreement, scooted back his chair from the table, and stated how living up there would be like being closer to God. Great Grandpa laughed and said getting higher on a mountain is not what gets one closer to God. What is in one's heart and the way one lives gets him closer to God. All chuckled and then nodded in agreement.

So, it was settled. Up into the mountains they would move their families. The men stood up, slightly stretched their backs, shook hands with each other, and placed their hands on each other's shoulders. The fire in the fireplace crackled and popped as if voicing its support for their decision, and its flames seemed to make the cross above it glow.

After a short break, the men returned to their places around the table. The table was made of thick timbers and was a heavy, stout piece. It had strength to it, just like the strength the family would need in their move to the mountains. That table had seen many a meal and many a discussion about family affairs. What it would see next was one of the most important decisions the family had yet to make. Great Grandpa and the men spent the next hour discussing which mountain to go to. One of the men noted that none of the mountains to the east of the valley were good choices. They were too close to the new settlers and their settlements back along the woodsman's blazed trails. Another man agreed and said going westward was their best choice. A brother mentioned that the western mountains at this end of the valley were also too close to the newcomers. The better choice would be the west mountains much farther down along the long valley where few people had been. Some of the men gently slapped their hands down onto the table in agreement. The fire crackled and the flames of the candles flickered a bit more brightly. The inside of the cabin seemed just a touch brighter now.

Great Grandpa arose from his chair, stood, and faced the fireplace for a moment. Everyone's eyes were fastened upon him. He inhaled deeply, looked up at the cross above the mantel, and turned back to the group seated around the table. Then, he looked into the eyes of each of his brothers, and then scanned the faces of the others. He cleared his throat and said when he and a couple of his brothers had been near that end of the valley while hunting, they would sometimes stop to rest and peer up into the grandness of the mountains beside them. It was peaceful, and had a sacred air about it. The brothers silently nodded in agreement. The other men sat motionless, awaiting more from Great Grandpa.

Great Grandpa proceeded. He spoke about how one mountain in particular stood out to them. It was taller than the others. The mountains on each side of it stood tall and sharp as if they were its flank guardians. Its peak seemed to always be topped with a cap of white snow. One brother added that the trees on the mountainside were so think they were like a green blanket gently draped over it. Another brother agreed and said the air there seemed more fresh than fresh. It was almost exhilarating inhaling the air in the breezes that gently flowed downward from the slopes. Great Grandpa spoke about two brooks that wiggled their way down through the rocks and trees, and their waters were crisp and clear. Both tumbled over some lower rock ledges and their waterfalls sprayed the air with tiny drops that glistened like thousands of rainbows floating through the trees on either side of the streams.

The first brother then mentioned that along the foot of the mountain arose some cliffs that seemed like fortress walls keeping the mountain safe from any outside intrusion. Great Grandpa noted that he and his brothers had not explored enough to find passes through those cliffs and on up into the mountain, but all were sure there must be one or two.

The second brother mentioned there was animal sign just about everywhere the men looked. Great Grandpa took another deep breath and looked back at the cross above the fireplace mantel. He said this mountain was beckoning them to come. The men around the table pursed their lips and nodded their heads in agreement. Yes, this would be the mountain to move to. It was almost a silly question, but one of the brothers asked if it was them choosing the mountain or the mountain choosing them! All had a good chuckle. The hour was late, and there was much to do the next day. Great Grandpa suggested the group meet again the next night to further plan the family move. Then, with goodnights, handshakes, and slaps on the backs, each went to his own cabin and settled in for much needed rest.

The next morning, each of the men shared with their families the decision to move, and to move up into the mountains far to the north and west of where they now lived. Although the exact date for the move had not been settled, the process of sorting through possessions and beginning packing them could now be started. There were many logistics to be considered and arranged as well, including obtaining the necessary wagons, stockpiling provisions, and dealing with livestock issues. Arrangements would need to be made for selling their properties. Discussions within family groups were held about preparing the planting plots, even though nobody really yet knew if they would still be there long enough to plant and harvest any vegetables or fruits for the year. Plans still had to be made to cover different contingencies and times for moving. If they were to move soon, they needed to be prepared for that. Whoever became the new occupants of the cabins and land would benefit from the work and plot preparations the family would make. If they were to move later, they would still need to produce the foods and other commodities needed to get them through the year. Putting such differing plans into place at the same time would be difficult and much work. It would be demanding. But it would prepare everyone for the journey forward and up onto the mountain.

 The snow had stopped falling early in the morning. The ground was covered with a fluffy white blanket that looked almost like wool. It was in sharp contrast with the dark brown of the cabin logs and fences. Footprints were scattered here and there through it, some from people and some from animals such as the rabbits and raccoons that wandered across the grounds in search of food. The sun rose high in the sky that day but failed to warm the ground enough to begin melting any of the snow. Its rays glistened off the snow like diamonds, and it made one's eyes ache to look out across it. Even though the snow held fast, there seemed to be a sense that the warmth of spring was not far off. The earliest signs were present. A few buds had emerged already, risking getting nipped by cold nighttime air. It seemed as if those buds were calling for the spring warmth to come and willing it to arrive. Each year as the spring warmth arrived, activity around the cluster of cabins would increase much beyond the slower pace of the winter months. But this year, at this time, the later winter activity was every bit as bustling as the family made preparations for their move.

As planned the night before at Great Grandpa's cabin, the men again gathered to discuss the move. The trails of their footprints through the snow seemed to make a web linking the cabins together. The wind had come up and was stirring the snow. As one of the men entered Great Grandpa's cabin, a lump of snow slipped off the roof and slapped him on the top of his head. He shivered and shook his shoulders, then stomped his feet to clear them of snow clinging to them. Many of the others experienced similar things as they made their way into Great Grandpa's cabin. The wind seemed to want to enter the cabin along with each of the men. With each whiff of the wind, the fire in the fireplace would shift and flicker. Candles were alight on the table and mantel, as well as in sconces along the walls. There was the slight scent of burnt candle tallow hanging in the cabin air. The light seemed to illuminate the men's faces with a dull yellowish hue. Each took his place around the large table, sitting down quietly and then speaking in low tones with his neighbor.

Great Grandpa cleared his throat and began the discussion. Decisions, he said, had to be made about the time to go. Decisions had to be made about what should be taken and what needed to be left behind. Decisions had to be made about where to go once on the mountain. One of the brothers cautioned they must make their move early enough so they could get new cabins built on the mountain before the winter snows arrived. That would be an imperative for their survival and success. All agreed. Great Grandpa noted that, considering the time required to build the cabins, arriving at their selected mountain site by early summer would be the latest safe time to arrive. As to what should be taken or left behind, those decisions would become clearer as the packing and obtainment of wagons progressed. It was the last of the decisions that seemed the most urgent to resolve: where on the mountain should they all settle?

Great Grandpa suggested he and two brothers go and find suitable passes to get through the cliffs and up onto the mountain. It was he and the brothers who were most familiar with the upper north valley due to their previous hunting there, and they already had knowledge of some potential good places to traverse the mountain. It would take too long for folks less familiar with the area to find their way there and back before the move had to take place.

All three brothers supported what Great Grandpa said, and some discussion amongst the group of men ensued. Nobody was in disagreement, and most of the conversation focused on the timeline to accomplish the tasks. Great Grandpa said the three of them would need to quickly explore the slopes and locate some good locations for potential homesteads. They could depart in two days after preparing themselves for the excursion, and hope to return as soon as possible with information the entire group could consider in making their final decisions about the move. Several of the other men stated that those who stayed behind would be in charge of coordinating and managing the tasks necessary for leaving the valley homesteads. Then, Great Grandpa said if everything went according to this planning, the family would be moving by mid-spring. He glanced at the cross hanging above the fireplace mantel, took solace, and smiled. It was a heavy load he and his brothers would be undertaking, but he had faith they would be guided by God to successfully manage it all.

CHAPTER 6

Finding the Mountain

Great Grandpa slipped his pack on over his shoulder. His thick coat cushioned his shoulder from the pack's strap, which was a good thing considering the weight of the provisions stashed in the pack. Although the last early spring snow had fallen at the homestead, the air still held a bite to it and could freeze one's exposed skin. The thick fur of his coat would keep Great Grandpa insulated from the stabs of the cold air. The pack had been filled with provisions to enable Great Grandpa to be away from the homestead for a couple of weeks. He shifted the pack around a little to get it more centered on his back and said a little "humpf!" as the pack moved. Then, he checked his belt, tapped his boot, and adjusted his hat. Time to go! It was time for he and his brothers to set out on their trek to the north mountain.

The three men met in front of Great Grandpa's cabin and grabbed each other's shoulders in a greeting. They smiled at one another and turned to face the path that would take them away from the homestead and off toward the north. Small clouds condensed in front of their mouths and noses as they exhaled. A thin blanket of snow remained on the ground. The wind had fortunately subsided. The morning was still and crisp, and sounds seemed to carry a long way with a sharpness that alerted the senses. Great Grandpa smiled, pointed his walking staff toward the north, and told his brothers it was time for finding the mountain! The phrase "finding the mountain" meant getting to the mountain and finding a way up onto it and locating suitable homestead sites. The brothers nodded their heads, and all three took their first steps away from the homestead.

Going north through the valley meadow seemed to be the easiest way for the three men to make their way northward. Most of that path would go through tall grasses and avoid fallen timbers and large boulders. There would be enough of those things to contend with later. With each step, the grasses gave up their coatings of frost and snow as the men's clothing brushed through them. The path they had walked looked darker than the surrounding grasses because of that. Grass crunched with each step they took, seeming to speak in a harmonious way with the "brush" and "swish" sounds of grass against the men's boots and coats. Once in a while a startled rabbit would jump out of their way and rustle the grass. And once in a while the men would be startled by a bird that suddenly flew up out of the grass scolding the three for disturbing their nestled places in the meadow. It was cold, and none of the creatures seemed to want to move. They wanted to hunker down and keep warm. Keeping warm in their cabins would have been nice that morning, but the three men had a task to accomplish, and staying in their cabins would not help get it done.

Their passage through the meadow was relatively easy compared to other parts of the trail that still stretched before them, but even so the combination of the cold and the grasses pulling on their legs began to tire them. After a few hours, it was time to stop and take a brief rest. Great Grandpa didn't want to rest for long. It was their body heat that helped keep them warm, and sitting still too long would let their bodies cool too much. Then, it would be more difficult to get warm again. So, their brief respite was just long enough to have some drinks of water and a chew on some jerky. The three sat down in the grass, and then laughed when they realized the grass was so tall none of them could see the others' heads. Each could talk to the others but couldn't see their faces. At the urging of Great Grandpa, the three stood up and brushed the grassy-frost from their arms. Onward they went.

It wasn't long before Great Grandpa and his brothers came to a stream that had cut across that part of the valley. This was a sign they were nearing the part of the mountains where they would turn westward and soon thereafter be in the foothills. As they neared the stream, they could see the meadow grasses becoming peppered with other plants that relied more on the moisture in the soils bordering the stream. Most were slumbering in the cold and awaiting some warmth so they could blossom forth and decorate the meadows. Great Grandpa could see some wild lupine, and could imagine its clusters of blue, pink, and white blossoms. There was some primrose here and there, wild garlic, and the ubiquitous black-eyed Susan and littleleaf buttercup. It would not be long until the butterfly weed sprouted its yellow and orange blossoms, as well. Great Grandpa saw the long, slender stems of some goldthread, although it was too early in the season for their white blooms to be out. But their glossy evergreen leaves were easy to spot. He thought it interesting to see so much of it but was thankful it was there. It could be used for medicinal purposes to treat wounds and sores, and even as an eyewash. Its roots could even be used to make a yellow dye useful in making clothing more colorful than the usual dull browns other natural dyes provided.

Once the snows were gone and the soils warmed, the meadow would be a glorious and colorful place. In the stream itself, the water trickled along over the rocks in the streambed and made them shine in the sunshine. Over many years, the running water had rounded and smoothed the rocks, allowing them to show the tiny crystals and veins of color that ran through them as if they were competing with the colors of the flowers yet to spring forth. The sound of the water was inviting, but it was icy cold and the three men wanted to avoid getting wet. They paused for a few minutes and looked upstream and downstream for a good place to cross.

One of the brothers asked if it was even necessary for them to cross to the other bank and wondered if they could just follow this side of the bank back upstream until it reached the point it flowed out from the mountain. Great Grandpa straightened his back and looked further up the valley. He shook his head "no" at his brother's suggestion. The mountain they were going to was still up ahead, and they wouldn't get to it unless they crossed the stream. And it was important that not only did they need to find a place to cross but that the place be one where the family's wagons could cross, too. They needed to find a ford somewhere nearby.

One of the brothers suggested they separate for a brief time, one going upstream and another downstream to search for a good crossing point. The third should stay where they were now and be in a position to help either of the others if the need arose. All agreed, and Great Grandpa was the one to stay.

The others departed and it was not long before both were out of Great Grandpa's sight. Great Grandpa sat down on a flat rock next to the stream and peered down into its waters. The glistening of the sun on the ripples and flows seemed almost hypnotic. He began to imagine the glistening of the sun on the waves of the ocean when the family fled England and sailed to the New World. He imagined the glistening of the sun on the waves along the New World shoreline where their colony had been established years earlier. The water-glistening could be deceptive. It could catch one's eye and distract one from being attentive to what was happening around him. It was more important to keep track of the sun and how it was guiding one along the way, much like the Son guides one along life's way. Some of the way is easy, but there are often unforeseen diversions and roadblocks that need to be overcome. Staying true to The Path is the only way to safely reach Home.

With a start, Great Grandpa broke his gaze from the water. He looked up and back toward the south to find where the sun was at in the sky. It had risen much during the day and was now at its highest point in its arc across the sky. Noon had arrived. Great Grandpa knew he and his brothers still had a good distance to go before the sun set for the day.

It seemed like a good amount of time had passed before one of the brothers returned and rejoined Great Grandpa. He had been upstream and had failed to find a good crossing. The stream was deeper up there, and rockier. The waters were rougher, as well. There were a couple of places where crossing could be done, but it would be risky for wagons, and it could be dangerous for children and animals. Great Grandpa fainted a frown. There would hopefully be better news from the other brother once he returned. That happened a short time later.

Not too far downstream, the stream widened and became very shallow. The water wasn't flowing too quickly there, and there were not too many rocks that could cause problems for wagon wheels. The stream bed was a bit muddy, and that could pose a little problem if wagons went too slowly or stopped midstream. The wheels could sink and then pulling the wagons out of the muck would be very difficult. Getting to that crossing would take everyone a few miles to the east of where they really wanted to be, and it would cost them about a day's journey going first east to the crossing and then back west to rejoin the northward trail. But it would probably be the safest way to go. The three men discussed the options as they ate a lunch and decided the downstream route would be the best choice.

By then, the day had passed into early afternoon and the air was warming. It was certainly time to shed the heavy coats. Each of the men removed lighter coats from their packs and then rolled and stuffed their heavier coats back into the same packs. The day was wearing away, and there was much territory to cover before settling down for the night. Great Grandpa stood up, slung his pack onto his back, and with a quick tilt of his head motioned toward the downstream route. The brothers got up, put their packs on, and the three resumed their trek.

The downstream crossing looked just like the brother had described it. Getting to the other shore should not be difficult for any of the men. As they stepped into the water, the muddy bottom oozed up around and then over the toes of their boots, but not much further. It seemed the mud was actually not thick and the bedrock beneath it would provide excellent support for wagons. As the men walked slowly across the stream, the water gradually rose until it was just beneath their knees. Their waterproofed boots kept their feet dry, and the only soaking their clothes received was from the splashing of water as their legs splashed through the flowing stream. They quickly found themselves on the opposite stream bank and then turned back to the west on their way to the mountain.

The afternoon part of the trek was much like that of the morning except for the warmth of the air. The day's sun had heated the air and the snow that once blanketed the ground was now gone. The top of the soil was still moist from the melted snow. The dry meadow grasses now seemed to capture and hush sounds moving across them. Aside from the three men's walking, it was the sound of the breeze rustling through the grass that made the most sound now. The mountain Great Grandpa had targeted was still much in the distance. He thought about how something that big could seem so close yet still be so far away. They could see it more clearly now, yet not touch it. There would be yet another day's walk – perhaps two -- before they reached the foothills at the base of the mountain. The late afternoon sun made the outline of the mountain more easily discerned, yet the peak was far enough away that details on its slopes were not clearly distinguishable.

A slight darkening of the sky began much too early for Great Grandpa and his brothers. The sun was low near the horizon, and its light was beginning to fade. It was best to stop and set up camp for the night while they could see what they were doing rather than bumbling about in the dark trying to do it. Besides, they had walked a long distance that day, and they were getting tired. Their legs were especially tired from pushing forward through the tall meadow grasses that grabbed, pulled, and resisted each step they took.

The men chose a spot to camp that was on a slight rise above the rest of the meadow floor. Each quietly groaned as he slipped off his pack and lowered it to the ground. Great Grandpa stood straight, arched his back and stretched as soon as his pack was down. He took in a deep breath and gently smacked his chest with both hands. One of the brothers abruptly sat down next to his pack and slumped forward a little. There would be no fire that night since there was not any wood nearby that could be gathered and used for one. It was what was called a "cold camp." That was an apt name because the night air would cool quickly and the camp would be cold through the hours just after sunrise the next day. The threesome ate a quick meal before the darkness wrapped itself around them.

There was a new moon that night, so the men would not have the benefit of its light to help them find their way around camp. They bundled themselves in their heavy coats, covered themselves with blankets, and laid their heads on their packs for a night's rest.

Great Grandpa awakened in the morning as the first rays of the sun crept over the crests of the mountains far to the east. Its early rays tickled at his eyelids, teasing him to arouse from his slumber. There was a thin layer of frost on his blanket and coat, and it was easily shaken off as he sat up and started to stand. His stomach rumbled softly, reminding him of the need to feed it with some breakfast. Some hot meal or eggs with ham would be good that morning, but he had no eggs, pots, or even a fire to heat them with. Cold preserved meat and some biscuits with a lard layer sandwiched in it would have to do. At times, such a feast would not be very appealing, but he could do worse and getting it into his stomach would be a welcome event. Great Grandpa nudged each of his brothers with the toe of his boot and jostled them to get up. The two brothers grumbled. One turned over and pulled his blanket more tightly around his shoulders, resulting in yet another toe nudge from Great Grandpa. By the time the three had eaten their breakfast and refilled their packs, the sun was a couple of finger widths above the eastern horizon and the cold of the morning air was giving way to being just chilly.

The path northward that day was much like the path that had been traversed from the south the day before. However, there was not another stream to cross and the grasses began to thin a little. By afternoon, the meadow grasses were becoming populated by more daisies, black-eyed-susans and buttercups, as well as scattered small trees, particularly red cedar. That was a sign Great Grandpa and his brothers were nearing the mountain. Red cedar seeds would blow down from the mountain slope and onto the valley meadow below, take root and begin to grow. It was a natural progression that would continue with the forestation of the valley unless there was a wildfire to burn out the cedars and restore the grasses. Great Grandpa was grateful that he and his brothers were making this trek at this time of the year before the later spring and summer storms started rolling through. Wildfires often started from lightning strikes. He did not relish the thought of running from a wildfire coming down through the valley meadow.

As the afternoon waned, the mountain was looming ever closer and the ground of the valley floor was becoming rougher and strewn with more rocks. Wagons could traverse it, but it would be hard on the wheels and axles. It would be better to walk than ride on the wagons so as to avoid the jarring of one's teeth whenever a wheel met a rock and bumped forcefully on it. An hour further along, the three men came to another stream cutting its way down out of the mountain. It was a rougher stream than the one they passed through the day before. The water seemed to be trying to shove aside the rocks in the stream bed, foaming and churning white in spots. The noise was certainly louder than at the first stream, but it was not a loud roar. Finding a crossing to the other bank would be more of a challenge this time.

The three men decided to use the same strategy hunting for a crossing that they used the at the first stream. But this time, Great Grandpa took the upstream path while one of the brothers stayed. As Great Grandpa walked along the stream bank, he watched the water as the stream bed narrowed in some places and then widened in others. In the narrows, the water was swift and almost angry as it slammed into the rocks blocking its downward flow. The water appeared unusually calm in the wider areas. Great Grandpa thought those places might be good for wagon crossings, but it was difficult for him to tell how deep the water was in those places. Wagons could only get across water that was about waist deep. He was reluctant to step out into the water and try to cross in case he might fall and get washed downstream. It would be better to wait for a brother, perhaps both, to be there to help just in case something like that happened. So, Great Grandpa returned to their starting point and rejoined his brother. The second brother was in sight coming toward them from downstream. As he neared, Great Grandfather and his first brother could tell the second was dripping wet. Evidently, that brother had ventured out into the stream and failed to get across without taking a tumble. Great Grandfather and the first brother laughed, and then covered their mouths with their hands to hide their laughter from the drenched brother who would not have appreciated the humor in it.

There were no easy crossings downstream. The waters were not all that deep – just over the waist – but the rocks in the stream bed would make it almost impossible to cross wagons there. The rocks were packed together too closely to allow for any spaces where wagon wheels could go. Great Grandfather reported on his findings, and the three decided to go back upstream to further investigate the crossing he had found. Water was dripping of the second brother's clothing, but he said he wasn't cold and could make it up to the next crossing and back. They picked up their packs and retraced Great Grandfather's path, soon arriving at what might be a good crossing. Since Great Grandfather had found it, the other two decided he should be the one to venture out into the water. Great Grandfather voted for his wet brother to go since a second tumble would not really make him any wetter. But he was overruled, most vocally by the wet brother, and had to take his turn in the stream.

Great Grandfather took a couple of steps out into the water, stopped, and then turned back and returned to the bank. His brothers looked quizzically at him. He smiled and picked up his walking stick and returned to the water. Before he would take a step forward,
he would push the walking stick ahead and downward to see if there was a hidden hole in the stream bed that he might fall into. He was feeling his way across since he could not see what was below the surface of the water.

Poke, probe, and step. Poke, probe, and step. His going seemed slow, but it was methodical and saved him from plunging into a hole just off to his right. Eventually, he stepped out of the water onto the other side, turned, and smiled at his brothers. This would be an okay crossing for the wagons. Then, Great Grandpa stepped back into the water to return to the others. This time, he was not as careful with his walking stick, and the stream struck quickly. His foot slipped on a submerged stone, and down he went into the water. He came back up spitting out water and shaking his head from side to side to get water out of his eyes. The two brothers laughed until their stomachs hurt and their heads ached. It seemed the wet brother had the best laugh of all.

The sun was low in the sky by this time, and the three men gathered some wood they could use to build a fire. A fire this night would be good to illuminate the campsite. It would also be good to cook some food, and – of course – to dry out wet clothes. Evening fell, and the distant call of an owl could be heard. It would be another cool night, but the fire would help warm everyone. Jokes were passed back and forth between the three as the sun dipped behind the mountains to the west and stars started poking out of the darkness of the sky. It was still a new moon night, and the stars seemed extra bright without the moonlight competing with them. The quiet of the night surrounded the three men as sleep soon overtook them. Only the sound of the dying crackling of the fire disturbed the quiet. All slept soundly that night.

Great Grandpa was the first to awaken the next morning. The air was chilly, but there was no frost on his blanket or coat. The orange of the sun was growing to the east in advance of the sun rising above the east range of mountains. It was a beautiful time of the morning. Great Grandpa inhaled deeply. Time for the others to get up, too.

As he turned toward one of his brothers, Great Grandpa noticed something odd where his brother was sleeping. There was a large lump next to him. Great Grandpa wondered if his brother had a second coat that had slipped off during the night and was now crumpled next to him. As he took a step toward his snoozing brother, that lump moved. His brother did not. It was certainly the lump. At his next step, the lump moved yet again, and from one end raised a head. It was the head of a young cougar. Great Grandpa stopped and stared into its eyes. The two were motionless for a moment, and then the cougar stood up, arched its back and legs in a stretch, and walked off out of the camp without a sound. It had evidently wandered into the camp sometime during the night, drawn in by the warmth of the low fire and the brother's blanket, and decided to spend the night in comfort. Great Grandpa gently shook his brother's shoulder until he was awake, then did the same with the other brother. During breakfast, he told his brothers about the cougar. He laughed and said if the brother was so cold, he should have snuggled closer to the fire. The brother was not amused.

Breakfast was consumed along with jokes about the cougar. But down deep, Great Grandfather took it as a sign of their being in harmony with the land in that place. It was a place God wanted them to be in. After their packs were ready, the three were all set to resume their trek. It was just after a few steps when Great Grandpa stopped. He was looking slightly upward and then raised his hand and pointed forward. The brothers stopped, too, seeing the same sight. They had missed it late in the day yesterday when their focus was on the stream. And they certainly had not seen it that night, or during the early morning when their attention was on the young cougar. But before them was the mountain. They were at its foothills, and the mountain rose in majesty not too far from them. It was a grand sight. They had arrived, and now it was time – as Great Grandpa had said days before – to be finding the mountain.

CHAPTER 7

Through the Pass

The mountain was so much larger than any of the men had imagined it would be. From their experience years before coming to the valley, they knew mountains were big. Yet the one in front of them was much larger than those off to the east. As far as they could see to the north or south were the foothills of the mountain. Compared to the mountain, the foothills were amazingly small – both in height and width. It was like the mountain had sprung suddenly upward out of the valley floor.

The foothills were covered with some grasses and certainly rocks and boulders, but also with an increasingly-thickening coating of trees. There was a mix of trees there, including some red cedars and a lot of maples. There were some scattered oaks, too, as well as some poplars and ash trees. The band of trees seemed to abruptly stop at the base of the cliffs.

It was these cliffs Great Grandpa and the brothers had seen during their hunting trips and thought they looked like the walls of a great fortress. Crags and cracks could be seen in the limestone of the cliffs. The limestone had been lifted and tilted by some tremendous force from within the earth long ago. Large chunks of stone had split and fallen to the cliff's base over time, and an occasional tiny tree was clinging precariously to small ledges in the cliff face from where the larger stones had fallen. Off in the distance to the north was a place where water from a mountain stream was tumbling over a falls and plummeting downward to a stream that made its way out into the valley. From their base, the cliffs rose at least a hundred feet. It was intimidating. It would be difficult to climb the cliffs to get onto the mountain itself, and clearly impossible to get any wagons up there.

The only answer to defeating the defensive wall of the cliffs was to find a pass. A pass would be a break in the cliff face and allow the men to more easily reach the slopes of the mountain. There was no guarantee they would find a pass. There were just a couple coming through the mountains to the east providing access to the valley meadow where their homestead was located. Just two passes along a mountain range of a hundred miles or so. The chance of finding a pass through this cliff face was slim. If one could not be found, then the three men would need to come up with an alternative place for the family to move. That may delay their move for at least another year.

Great Grandpa and the brothers discussed a strategy to use in searching for a pass. All thought it wise to stay together rather than separating as they had done searching for stream crossings. One of the brothers suggested they begin by going south along the cliffs. The sun shining on the cliff face might help them spot signs of any pass that might be there. All three agreed, and southward they walked, keeping close to the cliffs. As the sun crept higher and higher into the sky, its heat seemed to bounce off the cliffs and onto whatever was beneath them. The light yellowish-white color of the limestone was a good reflector of the sun's light and heat. It was almost hot by midday, and the three men were taking frequent breaks to rest and drink water. It seemed the further south they went, the more boulders they encountered and the more rugged the trail became. The cliffs seemed to become higher as they continued southward. By the end of the day, it was becoming obvious to Great Grandpa and his brothers they would not be finding a pass there to the south. So, they decided to return to their starting point to make camp and plan for the next day's search.

In camp that night, the light of the fire seemed to reflect off the rockface of the cliff. Some of the rock sat at angles that caught the light and shimmered like dim mirrors while some seemed to trap the light and create dark chasms. The rocks radiated the heat of the day's sun and kept the campsite warmer than the men expected throughout the first half of the night. If they listened carefully, they could hear the faint echo of their voices bouncing back to them from the cliff. One brother said it was almost as if the cliff was mocking them for trying to find a way through it. During supper, the three discussed going north along the cliff face. Great Grandpa thought that if a stream was making a waterfall up to the north, then it was more likely there would be other places – maybe some without flowing water – that could serve as passes. So, the three set their goal to reach the waterfall the next day and perhaps go a bit further north past it. Great Grandpa's sleep was not very sound that night as he kept dreaming about the cliffs pushing them back down into the valley.

 The next morning, Great Grandpa could tell the walk along the cliff face would be a warmer one than the previous day. The heat produced from the light from the early sun was already overtaking the coolness of the night air. Unlike the other two mornings, one of the brothers was already awake and rummaging around by the time Great Grandpa awakened. He was packing and looking for some firewood. The other brother was also awake, but had not yet emerged from his bedding. It was he who had the cougar cuddling next to him the day before. Without looking, he reached his hand to his side and patted the area to be sure there was no visitor there. Soon, the three were having their breakfast around the fire, with Great Grandpa facing the brothers.

 Suddenly, Great Grandpa became quiet and still. The brothers noticed and asked him what was wrong. He slowly tipped his head forward and told them to turn their heads slowly and look behind them. As they did so, sitting amongst the trees about a hundred feet behind them was the young cougar. It was quiet and watching them. As soon as it knew all three men were looking at it, it rose to its feet and walked away into the cover of the trees. One of the brothers seemed a bit shaken and wondered if the cat had been with them all night and was following them. Great Grandpa said it might be, but he took it as a sign they were there in harmony with the place and it was telling them it was where they should be.

As the three men made their way northward along the base of the cliffs, the sunlight seemed to be trying to reveal passageways into the limestone. There were a few passages, but they were small and relatively shallow. Certainly not passes to get up onto the mountain. The men noticed how there seemed to be a pathway through the jumble of boulders and rocks running parallel to the cliff face – even wide enough for a wagon to get through – but no pass through the cliffs up onto the mountain revealed itself. By noon, they had reached the waterfall. The falling waters roared and sprayed, and the sunlight passing through them made rainbows that seemed to frame the waterfall like an old master's painting. It appeared any one of the three of them could climb up the cliff and squeeze through a space between the rockface and flowing water and get onto the mountain, but that would not suffice for getting wagonloads of provisions and supplies, or many people, up there. Getting across the stream past the waterfall would be easy, even for wagons. Not far downstream from the falls was a nice ledge of rock just a few inches beneath the top of the water. Yet the men's search for a pass would need to continue. By mid-afternoon, the waterfall was well behind them, and still no pass was evident. As the three sat down for a rest break, one of the brothers said if this harmonious place wanted them to be there, it should be showing them the way to a pass by now. Great Grandpa just said there was more daylight left and they should not give up yet.

Not long after, one of the brothers spotted a deer standing in the trees ahead of them. It was obviously watching them but did not seem scared and stood its ground. As the men drew closer, they could clearly see it was a handsome buck. None of them had seen a buck that size before. Its coat looked silky and unblemished. It held its head high and its antlers seemed to touch the tree branches above it. The men stopped and stared, and soon the buck began to walk. It walked across the path the men would take ahead and then just far enough into the trees so it could still be seen and then stopped and looked back at them. It seemed to be waiting for them. Great Grandpa nudged the brothers forward and they walked slowly along the path. As they neared the buck, it began walking again, this time toward the cliff. The three men followed, slowly and carefully, keeping the buck in sight as they went forward. At some point, the men lost sight of the buck. They couldn't figure out where it had gone. Nevertheless, they decided to keep walking, hoping they might catch sight of it again.

Great Grandpa and his brothers didn't see the buck again at the cliff face. What they did see, however, caused them amazement. There was an opening between the rocks of the cliff face. The opening was broad, enough for two wagons to pass through side by side. The floor of the opening was covered with pebbles and no large boulders, and its upward angle was not steep. Great Grandpa and his brothers could see that its upper end opened onto the mountain. The mountain had revealed its pass to them! Great Grandpa smiled and said this place – that God -- wanted them there. Then one of the brothers pointed up the pass and called for the others to look where he was pointing. Up at the top end of the pass stood the large buck. It stood there looking at them for a moment and then turned and bounded out of sight into the trees on the mountainside.

CHAPTER 8

The New Homestead Place

Great Grandpa and his brothers could scarcely control their excitement. That night they would be camping on the mountain! They made sure their packs were secure and began their walk up the slope of the pass. The limestone rocks on either side of the pass looked as if they had been cut flat with a saw. Great Grandpa thought the rocks must have been cut by the hand of God Himself. The mineral grains within the rock of the walls glistened on the north face as the sun's rays struck them. It was almost as if the pass wall was covered with jewels. The south face was in shadow, but even then, the tiny crystals in the stone glistened from the light reflected from the opposing cliff wall. Once above the cliff face, the path of the pass continued upward some distance with the sides of the mountain gently rising away from the path on each side. Just as Great Grandpa and his brothers reached the very top end of the path, the sun was almost touching the top of the mountain as it started to sink behind it. There might be twenty minutes of light left to set up camp. All three of the men were smiling so much that Great Grandpa said it did not matter if the sun set on them because their smiles would be bright enough to light up the camp!

The night passed with Great Grandpa and his brothers having unsettled sleep. Their excitement at finding the pass was keeping them awake, and it was quite late before any of them finally managed to drift off into sleep. None were ready to roll out of their bedding that following morning. There was a light mist all around them. It was a mountain cloud that had enveloped them in those early hours. Staying in bed would feel good. It was cozy there.

Nevertheless, they forced themselves to get up and prepare for the day's exploration for a homestead site on the mountain. Once up and moving, things seemed to be accomplished with amazing ease. The three went about their tasks and in a short amount of time were ready to hike up onto the mountain. But where to search first for a homestead site was the question.

The three men sat down facing each other, with the two brothers' backs facing upslope and Great Grandfather's downslope. The three debated and each suggested going one direction or another and rationale for going that way. It seemed their discussions were just going around in circles, and after a while they sat in silence with their heads hanging down, frustrated with their inability to decide where to go. Finally, one of the brothers said they should just go straight up from their camp and see what was there, and then go south or north from that point if needed. Great Grandpa looked up, and with a smile said maybe they should follow the deer. The brothers raised their heads and asked him what he meant by that statement. Great Grandpa pointed over their shoulders, and as they turned to look, they saw the large buck from the day before. It was standing amongst some trees not far upslope from them, staring at them. All agreed that following the deer was as good a choice as any. One of the brothers joked that if they spent the day and didn't find a homestead site, it would be the deer's fault. The other brother guffawed and said if they didn't follow the deer and failed to find a site, it would be their fault. So, following the deer is what they did.

Throughout the morning, the deer kept its distance from Great Grandpa and his brothers, yet was always in sight. The buck wound its way through the trees and around boulders and ravines, but was always on an upward climb. At some point, the mountain mist seemed to clear, allowing the morning's sunrays to peek through the trees and dance on their faces. When Great Grandpa could catch a glimpse of the sun, he could tell they were winding their way slightly to the north along the mountainside. He couldn't remember when he had ever smelled air so crisp and fresh. With each breath he took, he felt more invigorated than he had for years. That was good since walking upslope was a tiring activity. It wasn't as tiring as climbing would be, and certainly not as dangerous, but it was demanding and worked leg, back, and abdominal muscles that usually had it much easier down on the flatter floor of the valley.

The path they were walking was rough and certainly not well-worn. In fact, it was not really a path at all. It was just spaces through the trees that wound between rocks and boulders. Small and medium sized stones tumbled downslope as the three men's feet dislodged them along the path. The rocks' clattering sound echoed around them. Great Grandpa wondered how the buck managed to move so quickly – and seemingly effortlessly -- without disturbing the rocks.

The rock outcroppings on the face of the mountain glittered from sunlight touching the angled surfaces of minerals in them. Some of the rocks had darkened from weathering and had a dull sheen to them, while others were bright and clean – evidence of more recent cleaving when some weathered rock separated and fell off downslope. Great Grandpa had to alternately open his eyes wider and then squint as he moved from the shadow of a tree into a patch of bright sunlight and then back into another tree's shadow. He could feel the coolness of the mountain air on his face when in the shadows and the warmth of the sun each time he left a shadow's zone. A light breeze kept the branches of the trees rustling. Except for the occasional tumbling of rocks – and his own breathing -- it was just about the only noise Great Grandpa was hearing.

Life seemed to be emerging everywhere through the hardscape of the mountain. There were the trees, of course, and the buck. But there were also signs of other animals due to marks on the trunks of some trees, evidence of burrows amongst the rocks, or the flutter of bird wings. Grasses were few because of the rocks and the amount of shade cast by the trees. A couple of times, Great Grandpa stopped to take in the sight of a small, scrawny tree hanging on the vertical side of a large rockface, its roots clinging tightly to cracks in the stone. The base of the tree poked out from the cracks horizontally, and then quickly made an upward turn so the trunk and branches of the tree reached for the sky in a mimic of trees growing in more regular ways on the ground. Each tree had a thick coating of green moss growing on its north-facing side. It made the trees look as if they were made of soft green felt rather than wood.

Scattered across the thin soils between the trees were plants Great Grandpa had seen on other mountains in the past. Yet they seemed thicker and more robust here than on those other mountains. He could see the clover-like leaves of the wood sorrel, but its white and pink flowers wouldn't appear for several weeks yet until there was more warmth on the mountain. There were the heart-shaped leaves of dewdrops and false violets, some bluebead lily which would be waiting until summer to bring out its blue-colored berries, some garlic mustard, and purpleflowering raspberry. Tucked here and there was some cucumber root and hobblebush. Great Grandpa was glad there wasn't much hobblebush. It was aptly named because its stems hung close to the ground and their tangled masses made it difficult to walk through them.

Great Grandpa smiled when he spotted the heart-shaped leaves of some foamflowers. He always thought about walking into a cluster of them and reclining for a nap. Their small, white feathery flowers stayed close to the ground and looked like a white froth that would wrap around and cushion one's body better than the best mattress. Great Grandpa thought about how many of the plants there could be used for food or medicines, and it seemed interesting how many of them had heart-shaped leaves or blossoms to remind one of the love God held in His heart for each person. Great Grandpa thought that even though this place had a hard side to it, life would not be denied. God had created this place, and He created life to live on it. Great Grandpa felt as if the mountain was opening itself and offering to allow he and the family to become part of that life. There was much there to sustain them.

Before Great Grandpa realized it, noon had arrived and it was time to stop for lunch. A large flat ledge of rock presented itself not too far from where he stood, and he called to his brothers to meet there for a break. As the three men sat there, they kept looking around at the sights of the mountain. Above them, the skies were the clearest of blue. Icy whisps of clouds they called horsetails seemed to brush across the highest part of it. Those always were a sign of cold air, so Great Grandpa knew the warming time was still a few weeks away. Below them, a blanket of clouds was hiding the cliffs from their view. Indeed, the men were above the clouds, moving onto more lofty heights. They had passed through forest with a wonderful diversity of trees, with poplars and maples lower, and then more oak and ash. As they looked far upslope, they could see the faint line where the pines and spruces became the predominant species. Above the pines, almost too far up to see well, they could make out the bright whiteness of the snowcap that topped the peak of the mountain. This place – this mountain – was the kind of beautiful place that only God could create. Everywhere they looked, the three men could see His brushwork and handiwork.

Great Grandpa stood up and said they were burning daylight, and there was much ground yet to cover. One of the brothers said they needed to find the deer so they could find out where they would be going next. Amazingly, the deer had been waiting for them in a cluster of trees slightly upslope and to the north of them. The three men followed the buck for another hour before suddenly losing sight of it. That surprised them because all three were excellent trackers. They looked around the area but could not see the buck anywhere. The second brother said it looked like the deer had left them to be on their own for now. Great Grandpa walked ahead to the spot where they had last seen the buck. There, he stood in silence, looking past the tree cluster. He didn't move. The two brothers wondered what might be wrong and ran to join him. Once they joined him, they saw what had stopped Great Grandpa, and it stopped them as well.

Just past the cluster of trees was a huge niche in the sidewall of the mountain. It looked as if there were arms of the mountain enfolding a special area to protect it. At the far side, an arm wrapped itself around the niche and protected it from harsh north winds. The ground from the tree cluster took a gentle downward slope. Opening at the bottom of the slope was a more level flat expanse that was blanketed with trees and plants. The trees there were so thick they were almost like the grasses down on the valley meadow, and plants covered the flat of the niche like a carpet. There were plants that would bear not only flowers, but also berries, medicines and dyes. Water bubbled out of a spring just to the other side of the level area and gave birth to a shallow flow that quickly turned into a stream trickling down the mountainside. This place, Great Grandpa and the brothers knew, was the site for the family's new homestead.

The rest of that day and through the next, Great Grandpa and his brothers explored the new homestead site. It had everything the family would need, and was much more than any had expected to find.

It was a Godsend. Water bubbling up out of the spring was cold and pure with a clean taste, a rarity that settlers back to the east would call "sweet water." All settlers longed to find sweet water. It was always a sign of a good place to live.

Animals would venture through the niche, pausing to examine Great Grandpa and his brothers and then moving along their way as if the men were just a natural part of the scene. Squirrels stayed amongst the limbs of the trees and chattered at the men. Great Grandpa wondered if the squirrels were expecting him to talk back to them. Rabbits kept close to the base of the trees, and some raccoons would line themselves along one edge of the area, raising themselves on their haunches as if standing to see the men more clearly. Once their curiosity was satisfied, they waddled off into the brush. Chipmunks darted to and fro, sometimes dashing beneath the men's feet as they stepped. One of the brothers looked like he was doing a dance to avoid stepping on one. A variety of birds sang their songs and chirped back and forth as if reporting on each move Great Grandpa and the brothers made. During the night, the welcoming hoots of some owls wafted through the trees and across the homestead site. And there was the distant yet distinct call of some wolves and the yowl of a cougar. This place was full of life. It was a place that felt blessed. It seemed to have a sacred feel to it. It would be a good and fruitful place for the family to live.

CHAPTER 9

Pulling Up Old Roots for New Ones

A month had passed since Great Grandpa and his brothers returned from their trek up north to find a new homestead site on the mountain. While they were gone, the family had packed away everything except for the bare essentials necessary to keep daily life functioning. There were times when someone would discover the need for an item that had been carefully packed, but rather than trying to find and unpack it figured out how to use other things as an alternative. The cabins seemed more crowded now with wooden boxes and crates pretending to be furniture. Some things could not be packed, and that included the foodstuffs in the storerooms and root cellars. The family had also done some early plowing of their small fields and pruning of fruit-bearing bushes and vines. Seed had yet to be planted in the fields, and there was some debate about doing it. The soil had been warming since the snows had long ago melted, and there would be a need for grain for the animals and for baking.

The timing of Great Grandpa's and the brothers' return was proving to be awkward. Should the family proceed with planting or not? If so, they would need to wait until some harvesting could be done. That would make their departure later in the year and expose them to early snows up in the mountains. If not, they would need to procure some grain from neighbors to sustain them on their move and during their settling in at the new homestead.

Great Grandpa asked the family to gather at his cabin to meet and make a decision about when to pull up their roots from the homestead and move northward. The gathering began after supper, and the sun had not yet set. Its red rays pierced the cabin's windows, giving the interior log walls the aura of being on fire. The stones around the fireplace had taken on an orangish burnished glow from the light that made its way through the window panes. The warmth of the day reduced the necessity of the fire being big, so it was reduced in size to just accommodate cooking needs. The chairs around the table were ready to seat the men as it had during the winter meetings, but they would not be used this evening. Instead, the men and women of the family would stand together around the perimeter of the cabin's front room. Everyone knew what needed to be decided, so the meeting would not take long.

The decision was to pull up stakes and begin the northward journey as soon as possible. The elders who had weather-sense believed the signs were for a late autumn and late snows, so that would afford the family more time to get the essentials of the new homestead established before the harshness of winter fell upon them.

Over the next few days, some wagons could be loaded with goods and provisions and begin the trip ahead of the rest of the family. It would be the group with those first wagons who would be responsible for clearing the wagon trail the rest would follow, to blaze the wagon trail up through the trees and across the mountain to the new site, and to begin felling trees necessary for building cabins. The remainder of the family, including the children, would bring the last of the wagons with them several weeks later. That would ensure time to make the final sales of their properties and animals that would not be taken along. There would be little grazing available on the mountain, so the number of oxen and cattle to be taken north had to be judiciously considered. The sale money would be used to procure grain and any other supplies needed to get the family through the autumn and first winter on the mountain.

Great Grandpa and his brothers were chosen to lead the first group northward. The wagons made progress much slower than when the three had first made their way to the mountain, and Great Grandpa found it necessary to remind himself to be patient with it all. The oxen could only pull the wagons so fast, and pushing them too hard would harm them. Many of the family members accompanying them did not walk as fast as Grandpa and his brothers, so that was another thing requiring additional patience. Finally, care had to be taken to not risk the wagons crashing into gullies or rocks by moving them too quickly. At times, one brother or the other felt his patience was running thin, and Great Grandpa would sigh and tell them he understood but reminded them patience was a virtue they must share with everyone on the trail.

When the group reached the first stream cutting across the valley, the blues, pinks, and whites of the wild lupine were in full regalia. There were early buds on the primrose, and the black-eyed-susans were smiling up at the travelers. The butterfly weed had sprouted its yellow and orange blossoms as they awaited the first of that season's butterflies and other insects that relied upon the nectars held within their blooms and those in the other flowers. The sunshine was seemingly reflected in the yellow of buttercups that were sprinkled throughout the grasses. And the goldthreads' white blooms seemed to outline the path the wagons should take to the crossing to get across the stream.

The stream waters were running clear and a little faster than several weeks earlier thanks to the melting of snows up in the mountains that fed them. The animals seemed to linger longer than usual enjoying standing and leisurely drinking in the stream. Great Grandpa decided to let them have their fill because they would be worked much harder once they got to the mountain and had to pull the wagons upslope. The crossing at the second stream was about the same, but the water at that crossing was a foot or two deeper than when Great Grandpa had traversed it before. Its water was moving faster as well and required Great Grandpa and the others to tie pull-ropes to the wagons to help stabilize them as each wet its wheels and underbelly in the waters of the crossing. When the group reached the foothills, the paths had to be more zig-zag than straight in order to get around stones and boulders too large for the wagon wheels to roll over.

By the time the group arrived at the pass, the decision had been made to have the wagons stay encamped at the bottom while some men went up onto the mountain to clear some trees and blaze a path along which the wagons could travel. That first night in camp, one of the brothers looked around for the cougar. The other brother was looking for the big buck. Neither was spotted, although the brothers felt the eyes of those creatures upon them. They laughed at themselves, and Great Grandpa told them they might see their old friends later up on the mountain.

Great Grandpa and one brother were the first to go back up through the pass and cut blaze marks on the trees that would need to be cleared to make the road for the wagons to pass through to get to the new homestead site. After that was done, a larger group of men followed and started to cut down the blazed trees. That work took several days, after which a couple of men descended to the camp to get some oxen to help with dragging the felled trees to the new homestead site. Once there, the trees were cleaned of their small branches, the bark removed, and then stacked in readiness for cabin building. Most of the men were focused on the trees, and paid little attention to the white and pink flowers of the wood sorrel or the blue berries of the blue bead lilies. The pink flowers of the wood sorrel were often missed, as were the purpleflowering raspberries. But Great Grandpa would sometimes have the men take a break and then point out to them the plants that spread out before them across the mountainside. He would remind them what the plants could be used for and said all should be thankful the Lord put them on the mountain. At one time, one of the men was hurrying down the road and decided to make a shortcut straight from one place to another rather than following the curve cut through the trees. He suddenly found himself tripping and tumbling from an encounter with hobblebush. Great Grandpa laughed and decided he should point that out to the rest of the men, too. He smiled and told them that if they wanted to entangle themselves with hobblebush, they should probably do so next to some foamflowers to soften their falls!

Great Grandpa and his brothers had been very careful to blaze only certain trees that would not only open the road for wagons but also be the best for building cabins. The result was a road that sometimes curved when it looked like it could go straight, but the men were practicing good stewardship with the trees. It also resulted in a roadway that somehow was more level and avoided steepness upon which loaded wagons might tip over. In the end, the rest of the men were grateful for that since it made moving the felled trees to the homestead site easier. As soon as the road was ready, word was sent down to the camp to have the wagons brought up to the homestead site. The trip from the campsite to the homestead site took less than a day, and soon everything the men had taken from the valley homestead was again with them on the mountain.

At the homestead site, places were staked that demarked where each cabin would be built. The cabin sites were chosen so none would be right next to another, giving considerable space between them. For each family, space was marked for a cabin as well as for other structures such as small barns, smokehouses, or root cellars. Cabins were given the first priority for construction. Brush and groundcover were removed to make pathways between the cabins as well as a pathway to the spring and stream. The trees within the boundaries outlined by the stakes were cut down, with the men making certain when one fell it would not fall against and damage other trees that were to remain standing. The trees were cut as close to the ground as possible, reducing the amount of stump that would need to be removed. Stump removal was always the most difficult part of the process and required several men, one or two oxen, ropes, and plenty of grunting and groaning.

    Each tree was addressed with care as if being honored for what it was giving up for the family. The small limbs were removed and set aside for firewood. The larger branches were then cut off and set aside for smaller future projects such as furnishings for the cabins. The main tree trunks were then prepared. Drawknives were used to scrape bark off the logs so the wood could dry and cure more quickly and not be as prone to rotting due to the bark holding in moisture. Broad axes and adzes were used to form some of the logs and cut beams and posts, and smaller axes were used to cut notches where logs would meet for corners. The notches were double dove-tail, ensuring there would be no slippage of a log out of its corner. So skillfully were the notches made that a knife blade could not be inserted between the logs. Logs were joined together with wooden pins carved from leftover smaller branches of the trees, particularly oak. Downward holes were bored with braces and bits, and the pins driven into them with large wooden mallets that had been made of white ash that could withstand repeated pounding. The men used oxen and ropes to heft each log into its place since most weighed many hundreds of pounds. Wherever a porch was desired, longer logs were cantilevered into place so they would extend past the outer walls and a roof could be put on them.

    Openings were left in the sidewalls for doors, windows, and also for fireplaces. Some settlers had been known to build their fireplaces from roughly stacked loose stones and the chimneys from wood branches. Great Grandfather believed this increased the risk of fire, and none of them could risk having their cabins burn down as winter drew closer and closer.

Not all the members of the family were just woodworkers. Some had experience working with stone. Near the back of the niche near the west mountain face at the homestead site there was an outcropping of stone that was suitable for fireplaces, chimneys, and foundations. The stone-crafters were given the task of cutting stone and placing it at each cabin's site as foundations before a single log was put into place. All the men knew the importance of keeping the wooden logs up off the ground to eliminate wood rot, and constructing stone foundations was a critical step in accomplishing that. The sill logs were then placed on the stone and leveled, and from there the other log courses were added and built up the cabin. More stone was harvested and used to build the fireplaces and hearths and later the chimneys. Hauling the stone from the quarry to the cabin sites was laborious, and putting the stones in their places was almost as difficult as getting the large logs up overhead into their places.

Although not always the case, the major structural framing of the cabins and many of the log walls were made from oak trees. Poplars were also used for wall logs and some interior beams in the cabins. Pine was split and smoothed and used for floors and railings. It was a rough smoothing since there were a number of cabins to be built, and final smoothing could be done later – even after the cabins were occupied. Red cedar was utilized for door frames and window frames as well as for shingles because of its resistance to moisture and rotting. Cedar logs were split and then cut into wide shakes for the shingles and smaller ones for overhangs. Longer pieces were used to form Vshaped gutters to catch rain run-off from the roofs. Maple was not used for the cabin structures, but when it was cut and saved it was set aside for making furniture and other such things later. Once the logs were in their places, the men mixed mud with grass and leaves to make chinking for filling the cracks between logs.

The men worked long days constructing the cabins and had yet to finish several by the time the rest of the family arrived from the valley homestead several months later. Everyone agreed that if winter set in earlier than expected, those families whose cabins were unfinished could stay with other folks. As more men arrived, they were put to work building the doors and shutters for each cabin and later turned their efforts to building small barns and other structures to accompany each cabin. The barns were built much in the same way as the cabins but without fireplaces and chimneys.

Building the root cellars was something different. Digging into the ground was almost impossible because of the mountain rock. After many days of frustration, the men decided to just remove as much soil as they could and then fashion thick walls against which they piled and packed loose soil. There were many details yet to be dealt with, such as smoothing floorboards and installing fireplace mantels, but the basic structures had finally been completed before the first snowflakes of winter drifted down from the mountaintop.

CHAPTER 10

The Stories of the Wood

Grandma's rocking chair creaked as she leaned back into it after finishing her last tale about the family coming to the mountain. Her tales had stretched over a full week of evenings, and entertained everyone during the cold dark evenings of the winter. The fire had gone down and needed stirring, so Grandpa got up and used the iron poker to enliven the flames. Papa grabbed two more short logs from beside the fireplace and gently laid them on top of the fire. As they heated, some sap hiding in their grain popped. As the fire grew larger, items in the room shifted out of shadows into the glow of its light.

The time was late and past when children should be in bed. Their parents had been so absorbed in Grandma's tale they lost track of the time. They hurriedly wrapped their children in their coats and shuffled them toward the door. Momma stood by the door holding a candle lantern to help the departing folks see their way past the door and out across the porch. The candle flickered, and Momma closed the door as soon as she could. She was glad she didn't have to face the cold walk back along one of the pathways to another cabin. As the door latch clicked, she gently touched a log in the wall and lightly slid her hand down it, her fingers absorbing the smoothness of the woodgrain in it. She thought of what Grandma had told them about the building of the cabins. She imagined how the family must have felt their first winter nights in this same cabin. It felt warm. It felt secure and safe. It was sanctuary.

The next morning was frigid and bitterly cold. North winds whipped around the mountain, stirring up snow that had fallen on it during the night. The sun was doing its best to brighten the morning, but the blowing snow caught its rays and diffused the light, causing near white-out conditions on the mountain's slopes. The homestead was fortunately shielded from the worst of the wind, but couldn't escape the coldness of the air or some of the blown snow that deposited itself against cabin walls.

In anticipation of the storm, some of the men fastened ropes from cabin to cabin, and from cabin to barn during the prior day. Anyone needing to go outside would be able to slide their hands along the ropes and be guided safely from one place to another without risk of getting lost in the blinding snow. It was an old but tried and true method for getting around in such weather. The livestock needed attention each day, so folks could not just hunker down in their cabins and wait out the storm. Extra firewood and water had been stockpiled inside the cabins the day before, as well, so the need to go outside was minimized.

Momma and Grandma sat next to the fire that morning while they worked their stitches on a new quilt. The quilt material's thickness rested on their laps, providing some extra warmth to their legs and feet. The material was little more than scraps of cloth that had been saved from clothing, sacks, or blankets that had worn out and could no longer serve their original purposes. The scraps had been carefully cut into similar-sized squares and triangles. Now, they were being connected together with homespun thread by the skillful hands of two of the best seamstresses on the mountain. Their fingers were deft and moved quickly and smoothly as each stitch was made. The stitches were tight and close and clean on the backside of the material, unlike those made by less skilled workers whose backside work often looked like a tangled mass of threads. A few of the younger girls sat close by, watching and learning the stitching and pattern-making with the material shapes, and trying their own hands at quilt stitching on some extra cloth scraps. Some of the girls were quite good already and with practice would soon be as skillful as Momma and Grandma. If not quilting, they would be spinning thread or patching clothing.

Papa and Grandpa were sitting at the large wooden table cleaning their muskets. Grandpa would look down into the barrel of his gun to inspect for any gun powder residue that might still be clinging to its inside after the first swab of cleaning. Papa was gently polishing the flint cock and hammer lock mechanism on his musket. Keeping the guns in good condition was important since clean guns fired better and more accurately when the men were hunting game. No one wanted to waste powder or ball because of misfires. The men were very accurate shooters and usually required just one shot to bring down a deer or whatever animal they were hunting. They only hunted when necessary to obtain some meat for the family and only harvested the number of animals needed to sustain them. Some of the boys watched Papa and Grandpa and once in a while would be given the opportunity to hold the gun stock and rub it with some oil to condition it. The guns were heavy, and there was no shortage of grunts from the boys when they first tried to lift the firearms.

By early afternoon, the storm was subsiding and folks were emerging from their cabins to tend to chores such as splitting more firewood, fetching more water from the spring, or tending to the livestock. The tracks of wild animals criss-crossed the snow-covered ground between cabins. Most were from rabbits or raccoons. The men always looked closely at them, however, in case any of the tracks were from cougars or wolves. Cougar or wolf sign usually meant those animals had been driven down from their mountain lairs in search of food, and the homestead livestock was easy food for them. When such tracks were found, there was extra guard duty that came with it to protect the livestock. Few were the times when anyone went out in pursuit of the predators since they helped keep other wild animals in check and were important to the health of life on the mountain.

It was well past mid-winter, and the number of snowstorms should be decreasing as spring approached, although it was still a couple of months away. Between the chores, the family would sit to warm themselves by their fireplaces and talk about what needed to be done as the spring thaws arrived, and what projects needed to be done in the summer. There was certainly no lack of them. There always seemed to be something needing to be done. The winter chores were usually accomplished relatively quickly with the many hands available. That left ample time for folks to sit together and make some music, spin tales, or have some reading. Usually, the readings were from the *Bible* since that was one of the few books the family owned. Books were a rarity for most families, even back in the Old Country. They were expensive, heavy to transport, and took up space often required for other necessities. And in reality, it was rare for people outside of the nobility to know how to read, so having any book in their homes was not likely. In that regard, the family was unusual. The knowledge of how to read had been passed along down through the family for generations, and children began early in life learning the skill.

As the early evening crept into the day, the family found itself once again gathering to listen to more of Grandma's tales. She was seated in the old wooden rocking chair next to the fireplace, gently rocking back and forth, holding a shawl around her shoulders. The rocking chair was singing its tune with each rocking. The children sat on the floor near Grandma or on the hearth so they could warm themselves. Some of the adults sat in chairs they had pulled away from the table or from along the sides of the cabin walls. Others stood, leaning against walls or the stones of the fireplace.

The fire crackled and gave an occasional pop. The smell of the burning wood permeated the cabin as did the smell of burning candle tallow. Papa grabbed a log from the pile next to the fireplace and prepared to place it into the firebox. He tilted the log and looked at its end-grain, and then slid one hand down the length of the log. Then he said there was nothing like good old ash to burn well in the fireplace. One of the children asked how oak burned. Then another asked how the other woods burned. Papa began to explain that each had their own way of burning, some burning slowly and others quickly, some hotter than others, and each having their own smell.

Then the question was asked about the wood in the cabin. The children wanted to know about the wood that had been used to build the cabin, and all the other cabins in the homestead. Grandpa began by telling them what the different woods were and what parts of the cabins had been made using those woods. That didn't seem to satisfy the children, and they asked other questions about the wood. Eventually, the questions focused down to, "What was the purpose of the woods before they were made into the cabins?"

Grandma saved Grandpa from trying to explain the purpose of the different woods. She began by telling everyone that they had learned about each of the woods in two ways. The first way was what had been handed down to them from their forebears about the characteristics of woods and how they could be crafted and made into wonderful things. In those ways, each kind of wood had a purpose. Sometimes, the purpose would be for shelter, another would be for furniture, and yet another would be for religious things like crosses, chests, and cathedral altars. The second way they had learned about the purposes of the woods was from what they had learned from their native friends who had helped them find their way into the valley meadow years ago. Some of those friends had made their way up to the mountain homestead and stopped for brief visits in years past, but none had been around for quite some time. Their presence was certainly missed. Most had moved further north or to the west. But while visiting at the homestead, they had admired what the family had done on the homestead with the wood and shared their stories about each kind. At that, everyone wanted to know what those stories were. Grandma creased her brow, looked up at the ceiling, and scratched her chin. She quietly said she would try to remember it all.

To their native friends, the land, the animals, the trees – and more – were gifts to them from the Great Spirit. Each thing had been infused with the spirit of life, and since that life was from the Great Spirit, each thing was, in its own way, sacred to the people. Anything that was considered sacred had to be honored, used wisely, and not unnecessarily harmed or wasted. Each time they took the life of an animal or a tree, they would pray to thank the Great Spirit for the gift, and they would pray to thank the animal or tree for giving its life for them. For the native friends, the Great Spirit had given each kind of animal and each kind of tree its own special characteristics and its own special uses. It was wrong to misuse anything or use it contrary to the purpose for which it was created.

Grandma explained how this was similar to the way they believed. The family had for centuries held a deep and abiding belief in God, and it was God who created everything around them. Each created thing had a purpose, and that was to sustain the people and bring them closer to God. She continued by saying people were here as of God's creation, and it was up to them to honor and respect what God had created, and to use them in proper ways for correct purposes.

Then Grandma began to tell about the pines. Pine trees thrive in tough growing conditions. They should remind people they can also thrive in places and times when conditions are not good. Pines hold up well to heavy weight, are durable, and resist wear. That should also remind people that with God each person can bear up under the heavy weights of life and endure and resist those things that come to wear one down. At the same time, while pine is the strongest of the softwoods, it is easy to work with. If people are like the pines, they can be very strong, while also allowing God to work within them and shape them into the kind of people He wants them to be.

Then Grandma said pine trees can give us more than just their wood for building things, too. Their native friends learned to use the young shoots of pines, and their twigs, pitch, and needles, as medicines. Its pitch and sap could be made into poultices used to treat coughs and pneumonia. It could be put on the skin to heal boils, wounds, and sores, and help draw out splinters. That can be really important to those who work with wood! They learned to crush pine needles and mix them with hot water that one could drink in order to treat colds and coughs, croup and fevers, laryngitis and bronchitis, and even heartburn. Grandma told how their native friends viewed pine trees as symbols of longevity, wisdom, harmony, and peace. She said when anyone sees and uses pine, he or she should think about all that God has given them for healing. People should think about the wisdom they have from the guidance of the Holy Spirit. They should think about living in harmony with other people and with the things around them. And people should think about peace, how important it is, and everyone must sometimes struggle to obtain it.

Grandma was able to recall one story their native friends had shared with them. It was about some men of their tribe, long before people came across the great waters and began settling in the land. The men were seeking height so they could see above almost everything else in the land. They were seeking to be one with the forest so they could be in complete harmony with it. And they were seeking extremely long lives. After searching through the forests for some time, a spirit came upon them and discovered what the men were seeking. So, the spirit turned those men into the tallest of pine trees, within the thickest of the forests, and some of those trees have lived so long they can still be found in the forest to this day. Grandma then explained that although none of the family believed in such spirits, or in men being turned into trees, the story should remind everyone that God can change a person – not change as if into a tree, but change in the heart – that makes it possible for one to see God's way of life more clearly. It is God who raises each person to new heights and leads each person to the long life of the hereafter.

All this was very interesting to the children, as well as to the adults listening to her. Excitedly, some asked for more about the cabin's tree wood. So, Grandma sat forward in the old rocking chair, making it creak a long low groan, and said there is almost always more! She closed one eye and pointed her index finger to the side of her head. After a few seconds, she straightened and said she could tell everyone about poplar trees. One of the children exclaimed "popular trees," but Grandma corrected her and said it was poplar trees. And certainly poplar trees could be popular. There were giggles passing through the group on the floor. Momma hushed them. Grandma began by telling how poplar trees grow tall and straight, and that is like how God wants each of us to grow tall and straight in His ways. The trees are very strong for their weight, so people can use them as beams in their cabins and barns. So, even those in the family who are small and lightweight can be strong in their faith and in how they support the family. Poplar trees resist decay, and that should remind folks they can each resist the decay that sin brings with it as long as they follow what God teaches and always strive to live in His ways.

Grandma reached to her side and tapped on the cover of her *Bible* that was resting on a small round table next to the old rocking chair. As she tapped it, she said poplar trees existed back in Biblical times in the Holy Land, too. She said sometimes people hear of something called the "Balm of Gilead," and there are some songs about it. Those songs refer to it as something of healing from God. Then she said that was based on the balm's healing properties. The balm comes from the buds of poplar trees. Back in Biblical times, it was called Mecca balsam, and from it, people could get balsamic oils that were used to make balm. Balm was used to treat all kinds of ailments, including sunburn and cuts, as well as insect bites. It could be put on the skin to help heal sores and bruises. And it could help with bleeding, too. Balm was also be used to soothe painful joints and relieve chest congestion.

Grandma spoke of how their native friends knew about those same uses for poplar, although she didn't think they made "Balm of Gilead" from it. Nevertheless, they knew about many of poplar's healing properties, and even used it to help with headaches. She said when anyone sees or uses poplar, they should think about the many ways God has provided for us to heal our bodies. We also must be mindful that God has provided people ways to heal their spirits and souls.

Momma told the children it was important for each of them to know about the trees and be able to use that knowledge for not only building things but also for healing their ailments. Grandpa added that in each season, some of them go out amongst the trees to collect leaves, or bark, or other things that they bring back and store so they can use them as medicines whenever needed. Grandma then spoke about how the healing properties of the trees were not just for physical needs, but also spiritual ones. Red cedar was a good example of that.

Red cedar was one of the trees used in the cabins. The family used it for door and window frames, for shingles, and other things. Red cedar is not likely to warp or crack, and Grandma said that should be a reminder that if people are like the cedar, they can resist evil and not warp or crack under its pressures. She then said red cedar is water resistant and its heartwood is resistant to decay. So when anyone uses cedar, they should think about how God gives each person strength to be resistant to the dark things in the world that seek to decay the goodness of the life God gave to them.

Grandpa then added that cedar is a softwood and easy to cut and shape and work with. As with pine, people should see cedar as a reminder that God can shape each person into what He desires, if people let Him work upon and within them – just like when the family works upon wood. Grandma also said she knew cedar was good to use when making musical instruments, and the family had some wonderful instruments they used to make beautiful music. She then said each person was one of God's instruments, and each person should listen to the beautiful music God plays in each one. As with musical instruments, what comes out of one will be different from what comes out of another. It is the same with people. Alone or together, the music that comes out can be so wonderfully beautiful.

Grandma then sat back in her rocking chair, closed her eyes, and inhaled deeply. She motioned for everyone to inhale deeply, as well. When the sounds of the inhales ended, she mentioned how cedar can give its cleansing aromatic smell to an entire cabin. It has a refreshing smell and removes unwanted odors. She shared how their native friends spoke of cedar's fragrant, aromatic smoke when they burned it. That smoke helped them clean their thoughts, and it helped them clean out emotions they might have of bad, hurtful, or harmful things that the dark world was all too ready to plant into their minds and hearts.

Grandma said that kind of cleansing was like the cleansing God wanted to do in each person. He always wants to cleanse people of the bad odors that result from the evils that try to constantly surround and penetrate into people's hearts and minds. When that kind of cleansing occurs, people can then smell the goodness of God. Grandma added that their native friends use cedar in medicine bundles and used its bark and leaves as medicines. She said cedar is so very important to their native friends for physical and spiritual healing. To them, red cedar is spiritually very much alive and has much power. In a similar way, everyone should always remember God is alive in each person and in all things, and His power is greater than any power that exists anywhere. It is His spirit and grace that gives people physical as well as spiritual healing and strength.

Next, Grandma told how some native friends would share stories of very old times when cedar smoke spoke to their people. It was a time when plants, animals, and people were all the same kinds of beings. They communicated with each other through a very old language that their minds had now forgotten. But that language could still be remembered in their bodies. Although their people cannot remember things from those old times, the smell of aromatic cedar smoke can bring forth those memories, even if the people are not able to put those memories into words. Grandma mentioned how God has put goodness deep into each person's heart and soul, and regardless of how one lives life, the deep memory of that goodness is still there, and it reveals itself through the ways we treat each other and how we revere God. She also reminded everyone that there are times in prayer when one just doesn't have the words to express themselves, but they should always remember that the Holy Spirit can and does speak for everyone in those times.

Grandma closed her eyes again and took in another deep breath.

The old rocking chair gave a quick creak as she shifted her position on its seat. Some of the children shifted their positions on the floor, too, and those sitting on the hearth moved slightly away from the fire to keep from scorching the backs of their clothing. Then Grandma said there was even more about red cedar worth knowing. She told how important cedar was for their native friends as a ceremonial plant. They use it as a purifying herb and burn it in purifying ceremonies associated with prayer and healing. They associate cedar with dreams and protections from disease, too. Grandma said that should remind people that God can purify a person, and with prayer can bring healing. She added that their native friends consider cedar a symbol of generosity and providence. So, whenever a person sees, uses, or smells cedar, they should be reminded of God's providence and the generosity He has bestowed on everyone. People should also be reminded to be generous to one another as God is generous to them.

Papa asked Grandma about the oak trees. The family had used a lot of oak logs in building their cabins because of its strength and durability. The wood was hard and its close grain makes it dense and heavy. It also does not warp or shrink much, and it resists water and decay. Grandma agreed, and said oak also grows slowly compared to other trees. Its growth is sure and steady, and the trees stand strong in storms, perhaps moreso than other trees. She said that everyone should remember that if we abide by what God teaches, each person can be strong and durable in their faith. She also said most people grow slowly in their faith, and with God's hand can steadily grow in their spiritual strength so they can withstand the storms of life that come upon them. She said the native friends often spoke of oak as a medicine tree and considered it a sign of strength and protection. In many ways, oak trees protect other things in the forest on the mountain. In much the same way, everyone should always know that

God protects them.

Then Grandpa said they shouldn't forget about the white ash trees. Some of that wood was also used in the cabins. Grandma nodded her head "yes" and said white ash is much like oak. Surprisingly, it is even stronger than oak, has much the same graining and coloring as oak, but it is more lightweight. She said she liked the furniture that had been made with it. Grandpa added that white ash was great to use for ax and mallet handles and things like that because it could withstand the shock of striking other things and not split or shatter. One of the children asked if ash was used by their native friends for medicines like some of the other woods. Grandma responded that their friends told them it was, although she could remember few details about that. She did remember that some of their friends would chew raw ash bark as part of a hunting ritual, but she didn't know what that really did for them. And to her knowledge, nobody in the family had tried doing that. One thing that came to her mind as she was speaking was how their native friends believed ash was poisonous to rattle snakes and how they would make canes out of the wood to drive away snakes. One of the other adults shuddered at the thought of rattle snakes and said he was glad there were few of them seen thus far on the mountain. With a smile, Grandpa said it might be because of all the white ash trees growing on their side of the mountain. Everyone chuckled quietly. Grandma said all of that should remind everyone that God is always seeking to drive away evil and harmful things, and He doesn't rely only on one thing to help us in life. Sometimes, He leads us to something when one thing is not workable or cannot be found. She also said God has different ways, different things, that can make each person strong in His ways.

Momma said she liked the look of the maple wood in the furniture in some of the cabins. Its reddish-brown color was a nice compliment to the red of oak and the lighter colors of the other woods. Papa replied that maple is hard and strong and not as easy to work with as some woods, but it makes furniture that does not dent easily and it wears well. Grandpa agreed, but said it might shrink some and its coloring tends to fade if it is left out in the sunlight too much. Papa responded that at least the wood was resistant to decay. Grandma stepped in and said that is like God's work in each person, too. Through God's grace, each of us can withstand the dings and hits that come from living life, especially on the mountain or during difficult times like that last year when they were living down in the valley or when the past family lived in the coast colony.

Grandma smiled and said some of their native friends also use maple as medicine, particularly its bark. Not to be outdone, Grandpa said there was one more thing their native friends told them about maple trees. You could tap into a maple tree and get some of its sap, then cook it down and make a sweet syrup out of it. Momma said sweeter stuff was just about the last thing any of them needed! Then Grandpa said he could almost taste the taffy candy made from it right now! He closed his eyes and licked his lips. Some of the children giggled and licked their lips, too!

Grandma said their native friends considered maple sap a gift from the Creator. One of the native stories their friends told is how Sky Woman had two grandsons, one of whom was called Maple Sapling. Maple Sapling represented creation, life, day, and summer. His twin brother was called Flint. Flint represented death, night, and winter. The two brothers were constantly in opposition to each other, with Maple Sapling always trying to do good work in the world and Flint always trying to sabotage those works and commit crimes. This represented the existence of both good and bad in nature, but the two were in a natural balance with each other. Some of the native stories say humans were created by Maple Sapling and some were created by Flint, and that explains why humans can have both good and bad natures in them. Grandma continued by saying that was much the same in what one learns from scripture. People can behave both in good ways and bad ways. God teaches everyone to do good and behave in good ways and do good things, and Satan seeks to destroy and ruin anything good. In a person's life, there are almost always times when one's good nature is challenged by bad thoughts or ideas or actions that arise out of one's bad nature. Each person should always strive to seek the good, and resist the bad.

As with other story evenings, this one was getting late. It was time for the little ones, as well as the elders, to be in bed. Some members of the family were beginning to stand up and stretch. It was time to return to their own cabins. And Grandma needed to finish the evening's stories about the trees. So, she offered one last thing about them. She reminded everyone that, in many ways, trees were not only special to their native friends, but were also sacred to them. Trees gave of themselves for shelter, for warmth, and medicines, as the Creator had planned. And that was true for the family, as well. Trees were a gift from God, and everyone should always be mindful of how important that gift was. Everyone would pass that night within the comfort of that gift.

CHAPTER 11

Cross Wood

Several evenings passed without the family gathering for story time. Work during the days had been a little more taxing than usual, and getting to bed earlier each night seemed to be the best medicine for everyone. The earliest signs of spring were starting to show in some spots around on the mountainside, but the snowcap maintained its grip on the mountain top. The trees had not yet started to bud, but there seemed to be the sense of an awakening in the animals that roamed the forest. Grandpa called it the "pre-awakening." One could sense it coming, but it was not yet here. Grandma called it God's stirring everything back awake from its winter slumbers. It was in that sense that there was a pre-awakening in the family.

The cold mountain air still held its grip on the homestead, but the sky was deep blue and clear except for a few wispy horsetail clouds floating lazily past and over the peak. Papa and Grandpa had almost finished eating the scrumptious breakfast Momma had cooked when a knock on the cabin door startled them. Papa pushed his chair back and walked to the door, and after grasping the handle, opened it just a little to see who might be outside. He wanted to keep as much heat in the cabin as he could. Standing at the door was one of Grandpa's brothers. He had a serious expression on his face, but his eyes glinted with excitement. Papa ushered him inside so the door could be closed quickly. Momma invited him to sit down at the table and share some of their breakfast, but he declined, saying he had already eaten that morning. Grandpa folded his arms across his chest and leaned back in his chair, and asked what brought this brother over to this cabin on this coldly invigorating morning. Then he smiled.

His brother began by saying he had a dream last night. Momma said everyone has dreams. But the brother said his was not the usual or ordinary kind of dream. Papa leaned forward and asked what it was about. The uncle said he thought it was a message telling him the family needed to do something. Everyone looked puzzled and some mumbled questions. "What kind of message?" or "What were they to be doing?" Grandma shushed everyone and said there are just times when the good Lord speaks to us, and it can sometimes come in one's dreams. She nodded her head toward the brother as if telling him to continue. The brother said in his dream, he was told the family needed to build a family chapel on their mountain homestead. At that, everyone straightened up in their chairs and some tilted their heads in surprise. The brother continued, saying that in his dream, he had seen all the members of the family that were there on the mountain as well as some yet to come, and they all needed a special place to go during special times. Papa said he supposed they could build a chapel, but it would be best to meet with the other family members to discuss doing it. Building a chapel on the mountain would require careful planning and certainly extra work from everyone beyond what they normally needed to do on the homestead. All agreed, and Grandpa said he would call a meeting of the family for that evening. After that, everyone around the table arose and prepared to get on with the chores that awaited them.

That evening, as during story-telling nights, the family members came and gathered inside the warm confines of the cabin. It seemed as if it had been a long time since the family had held a meeting like this. It had been way back in the valley meadow homestead when they met to discuss leaving there and moving to the mountain. Family meetings meant serious business. Grandpa began the meeting by asking his brother to share with everyone the dream he had and the message that came through it. Some folks had quiet gasps, some tilted their heads as if waiting for more information, and others crossed their arms and inhaled deeply. A few quietly clapped their hands. Then came the expected questions. Could they do it? Where would it be built? How long would it take? What would they use to build it? People seemed to be talking in small clusters instead of addressing the whole family.

Grandpa tapped his knuckles on the table to get everyone's attention. Yes, they could do it. If they were able to find the mountain and then build all the cabins and other buildings on their new homestead, it was certainly possible for them to build a chapel. Papa inserted that how long it would take would depend on how much time each person could contribute to building it. Everyone needed to attend to their normal tasks and figure out exactly when they could tend to chapel construction. Somebody would need to coordinate the group for getting each step of the construction under way and accomplished. Everyone looked at Grandpa. He smiled and said he could do that! With regard to where to build a chapel, there was much discussion. Many places around the homestead were suggested. Each had its strengths. Momma suggested that several of them do a walk in the next few days to assess each possible building site and determine which one would be most suitable. That sounded like a good idea to everyone.

Then the discussion shifted to what would be used to build the chapel. Papa said there were plenty of trees available, just as there were for the cabins. One of the uncles then added there was plenty of stone available that could be used for a foundation and some of the walls. Another brother then spoke up and said he thought each family had some materials stored in their cabins or small barns that were left over from the first homestead construction, and everyone could take a look at what they stored to determine what could be taken out and used for the chapel. Grandma said she even knew that some of them had brought things with them from the valley homestead – and some from before that – which could be used if the individual clans were willing to part with them.

Excited chatter ensued, again amongst the smaller clusters of folks, and it continued on for quite some time before Grandpa managed to gain everyone's attention. Once all eyes were back on him, he said it sounded as if there were no objections to building a chapel on the homestead, and it was a worthy project that could be done over the course of the next year. Everyone agreed. Several men volunteered to scout around the homestead for a building site and report back to the rest of the family by the end of the week. With that, Grandpa adjourned the meeting, and folks walked to the door, some with arms around shoulders and some holding hands. Their excited chatter was loud, and as soon as the last of them had departed, Grandma put her hands up to cover her ears and said her ears wouldn't stop ringing from all the commotion until the morning.

Over the next few days, several men walked the length and breadth of the homestead seeking a good location upon which to build a chapel. Before taking their walk, they discussed different locations, and were able to rule out a handful of them for various reasons. The few that remained under consideration would require a visit. One of those remaining sites was where the mountain road entered the homestead. Another was next to the bubbling spring, and a third was back in the mountain niche where stone had been quarried for cabins' foundations. Building the chapel on the road site would place it in a prominent place that anyone coming into or departing the homestead would pass. However, it would be difficult leveling the ground there due to the slope of the mountainside on either side of the road.

Constructing the chapel next to the bubbling spring would pair the serenity of the spring and brook with that of the chapel. A couple of the men thought that would place the chapel just a little too far from the cabins and could potentially damage the spring. So, the men's attention turned to the niche.

The ground in the niche was already flat, and it was close to the stone quarry. Getting stone for the chapel's foundation and walls would be much easier there. The niche was also not far from the cluster of cabins, and a chapel there would be better protected from the weather that sometimes raged from the north side of the mountain. According to their promise, the men shared their recommendation with the rest of the family by the end of that week. The site was accepted, and work on the chapel's construction would commence as soon as people were available to begin.

Through the spring, men took their turns cutting limestone from the quarry and shaping the stone, after which it was carefully set into place to form the chapel's foundation and for a fireplace and chimney. The lightness of the stone's color was an uplifting contrast with the dark forest shade. The chapel's entrance would face the south. The foundation's footprint was somewhat larger than that for any of the cabins. As the foundation was being built, others ventured out amongst the trees and began harvesting those needed for the walls and roof of the chapel. Bark was stripped from the logs, and those to be used in the walls were carefully honed with broad axes so their sides were smooth and flat rather than rounded like those in the cabins.

By late summer, the outer portion of the chapel had been completed, and attention was turned to its interior. Throughout the early autumn, the wood craftsmen devoted their efforts to creating a fireplace mantel, seating benches with backs, and then an altar, and finally a cross to be hung above the altar. Others crafted sconces for candles to illuminate the chapel during cloudy days or nights.

The mantel was a singular piece of red cedar whose length ran the entire width of the fireplace. Grandpa joked that he could lay on it and use it as a bed because of its size. The piece of cedar used was as thick as the length of a man's arm from elbow to wrist. And although cedar is light in weight compared to most of the other woods, it took four men to heft it into its place on the fireplace stone. The wood looked as if it had been rough-hewn, yet was smoothed enough to reveal delicate carvings of lilies, bunches of grapes, and vines that snaked their way left and right across the mantel's length.

The family chose poplar for the altar. By cathedral standards, the altar was quite small. Even so, it took four men to lift and put into place the solid piece of six-inch thick poplar that was to serve as its top. The seams where pieces of wood met on the sides of the altar were so cleanly made that they appeared to be just lines of grain running through the wood. In the center of the front panel of the alter was carved a medallion depicting a lamb with a tilted cross behind it. That was reminiscent of medallions the craftsmen had seen on cathedral altars back in the Old Country.

The last woodcraft item to be made and placed in the chapel was a cross. It took quite some time for Grandpa and his brothers to search through the harvested wood to find just the right pieces for the cross. Part of their time was spent deciding on just what the cross should look like. Eventually, all came to the consensus that it should appear rough-hewn just like the wood that made the cross upon which Jesus had been hung. At the same time, that rough-hewn look would be gently smoothed so one's hand could easily slide down along its beam and post so it could reveal finely carved intertwining vines with tiny flower blossoms. When it was finished, everyone was astonished to see the woodgrain in the cross forming the outline of a man with outstretched arms. That image was not one the craftsmen had planned but had arisen out of the natural grain patterns of the wood. The grain also showed some natural coloring changes, with more reddish grains seeming to run from the image's feet and hands and a little from its right side. The rest of the grain had a golden-brown coloration.

A final surprise about the cross occurred when one of the family clans presented the rest of the family a bundle that had been shipped from the Old Country and kept safely wrapped in a thick padding of cloth and stored in one of their chests for many years. The bundle was carefully laid upon a bench next to the altar, and everyone crowded around it to see what would be revealed as the bundle was opened.

As the strips of leather were untied and slowly laid out, the edges of the cloth began to pull away from the bulk of the bundle. With slow and gentle fingers, the cloth was pulled further and further until the contents seemingly burst forth. It was panes of colored glass. Small panes, just about the length and width of one's index finger, showing the characteristic bubbles of hand-made glass. There were red ones, green ones, amber ones, two deep blue panes (the rarest of colored glass!), and – of course – several that were uncolored. The children squealed and some adults gasped at the sight. Asked where the rare panes came from, the only answer was they had been saved from left-overs when one of the Old Country cathedrals had been built so many years ago. They had been kept as treasures ever since. These colored panes would now be fit into a finely-crafted frame of rails, muntins, and sashes that would support each piece of glass. Then a window opening would be cut into the wall of the chapel, and the colored glass framework fastened into that opening. The colored window was placed in the upper part of the east wall above the cross, and during the mornings and early afternoon the sunlight could shine through the glass and fall upon the cross. As the sun's rays shifted through the window, they helped the cross give the impression that the figure in the woodgrain was subtly moving as if alive.

The final touches inside the chapel were made through the winter, and by the first of spring the edifice was finished. It was such a wonderful place, nestled in a beautiful location on a beautiful mountain. Everyone felt extremely blessed to have such a chapel within their homestead. It was during a story-telling evening that the family gathering had been moved out of the cabin and into the chapel. Grandpa and his brothers felt it a good time for everyone to be there to take in all that had been accomplished.

At that time, one of the children was staring at the cross and asked what kind of wood the cross had been made from. Grandpa answered it was made from cedar. That, the child responded, was not what she meant. She meant the cross where Jesus had been hung. All eyes turned to Grandma. She turned slightly on her bench, and with a smile said no one really knew for sure. Some people claim the crossbar was made from cypress. Some say the base of the cross, or the post, was made from cedar or pine for its strength. Some also say the inscription above Jesus' head was carved onto a piece of olive wood. Then there are other people who say the cross was made of palm wood. The palm was supposedly representing the "Palm of Victory," meaning the triumph of life over death. The cedar was supposedly representing the "Cedar of Incorruption" that tells everyone Jesus would not suffer corruption or decay of His body upon death. And the olive represented "Olive for Royal and Priestly Unction." That meant that Jesus was the Christ and King of all, that He served the role of the ultimate priest, and He instituted – or provided – the means for everyone to receive comfort and perfect spiritual health. And whoever touches a piece of that Cross, even today, can experience healing. Whatever wood that Cross was made from, it was made sacred by Jesus' death upon it.

Another of the children then asked why the chapel cross was called sacred by some of the family elders. Grandpa's brother answered. He explained the chapel cross is wood that mirrors or reflects the wood used in the Cross upon which Jesus was hung and upon which He bled and then died. Another brother added that since the chapel cross is now to be kept in a place of honor and respect, it will always serve as a reminder of the Cross of Jesus and used in sacred ways for prayer, praise, and worship. Grandpa then said that the crosses in their own cabins were blessed so many long years ago by a priest. It is before those very same crosses most say their prayers and reflect on the Great Gift Jesus gave everyone. Each of the crosses have been set aside for special use, and are therefore sacred.

One of the older children scrunched his brow and asked why adults in the family speak of the mountain trees as being sacred. Grandma and others in the family speak of the trees used to build their cabins as being sacred, but Jesus did not die on the trees of the mountain. Grandma paused for a moment, smiled, and her eyes glistened. Jesus, she explained, died on a cross made from the wood of trees. She then said that the wood from the trees is made sacred by the way it is used. It means everyone must dedicate themselves to respect them, conserve and protect them, and not abuse them, but use them for purposes of good. Using them for purposes of good is using them as God intended. It is a way to set the trees aside for a special use. That use respects the sacred and high value of giving and sustaining life for all of God's creatures. Doing that brings each person closer to God. And getting closer to God is becoming more holy. When one uses something in a holy way, it becomes sacred through that use.

The quiet of the night settled onto the family in the chapel. The wind outside was still. The forest animals were silent. The loudest sounds were the breathing of people, the occasional creaking of wood in the benches as folks shifted position, and the soft crackling of the fire in the fireplace. The sconce candles flickered, casting their light across the room. And as that flickering light brushed across the cross, the figure on it seemed to move as if alive. It was sacred.